Louis Veuillot

Stephanie

The Story of a Christian Maiden's Love

Louis Veuillot

Stephanie
The Story of a Christian Maiden's Love

ISBN/EAN: 9783337258917

Printed in Europe, USA, Canada, Australia, Japan

Cover: Foto ©Andreas Hilbeck / pixelio.de

More available books at **www.hansebooks.com**

STEPHANIE

The Story of a Christian Maiden's Love.

— BY —

LOUIS VEUILLOT.

TRANSLATED FROM THE FRENCH.

NEW YORK:
P. J. KENEDY,
EXCELSIOR CATHOLIC PUBLISHING HOUSE
5 BARCLAY STREET.
1887.

PREFACE:

EVERYBODY reads stories. The little children have their tales of adventure. The young and the middle aged are fond of novels. The old pore over historical romances and enjoy the caustic pages of the satirists.

With the majority of readers, this taste for fiction is not regulated. It has become with them an insatiable passion. They cannot fix their minds on solid works. They must have stories, and as soon as they finish one they begin another. The supply equals, if it does not exceed, the demand. Authors and publishers are kept busy, and in the course of every year an enormous number of these books are issued.

But not only do the lovers of imaginative literature read too many novels, but they unavoidably get hold of some that should never have been written. And their liking for exciting volumes increases at a steady pace. They speedily acquire a distaste for "The Vicar of Wakefield," "Paul and Virginia," "Fabiola," and the like, and find pleasure only in the description of the workings of the most intense passions in the most fiery circumstances. And the writers, who must please them, in order to procure a market for their literary wares, make their plots more intricate, their incidents more sensational, their villians more depraved, their scenes more gross, and the whole character and influence of their productions more and more contrary to Christian principles and practices.

Novels are to be seen everywhere, and no one can pick one up at random with the certainty that he will not be shocked, and disgusted, and scandalized at its narrative and ethical teaching.

In these days, then, of demoralizing tales, it is a comfort and a delight to get hold of this exquisitely pure and wonderfully interesting story of " Stephanie." It is a prose poem. It is the emanation of a tender heart, clean and clear, and whether in the hands of gentle maiden or aged grandsire, no one can read it without being the better for it.

STEPHANIE.

PARIS, MAY 1st, 1820.

AND so all my planning is crowned with success: my own darling Elise, you are married, and very, very happy. How sweet it is to me to think of your happiness, and what a fair picture it is that rises before my mind at this moment; that beautiful old chateau of yours, with the bright, fragrant garden, and the old court where the grass grows, and the broad cool meadows, spreading away down to the rich knot of trees, where every tint is aglow in the warm light of the summer sun dying behind; for I always fancy you on these lovely evenings standing with your grave husband admiring the scene which lies before you in its calm loveliness, a perfect picture of your own peaceful lives. Ay, peaceful, peaceful; how glad I am that

God has always given you peace, Elise, it is one of the greatest blessings He has to give. My castle-building head conjured up all this long ago, and now I contemplate my little tableau with the greatest complacency, as if it were all my own work. I fancy that when my two friends thank Providence for their happiness, there goes up a blessing for Stephanie also, as though she had really something considerable to do with it. That happiness is so precious to me, dear, that I love to hear you say I assisted it ever so little; but, then, I always prophesied good things of you, because you were so wise, and gentle, and brave. I chose you for my friend and confidante because you seemed so calm and strong that I could lean on you, and so loving, too, that I could pour out all my heart to you, its folly as well as its wisdom, and trust that as long as you were your own dear self you would continue to love me and listen to me; and every assurance of your truth and friendship is a new joy to me. In Paris, somehow, people do not seem to feel like this. It is not friends that one lacks, nor caresses, nor confidences, but friendship.

Friendship we had in the convent, and I think she may be found out in the country's fresh green heart, but in Paris people do not seem to look for her, or wish for her; so I am very happy in having you to write to and confide in.

Now, I know that you are expecting me to begin and talk about myself, but I have really nothing to tell. I think I have said all there is to say when I have spoken of the real joy that comes to me in the reflection of your happiness; but about myself there is really nothing to tell. I am writing in the boudoir where you and I have so often been together, and there is no change except the one great change, that you are not here. The sun comes again to play on my window, and send the shadow of the ivy-leaves quivering on the floor; out in the garden the limes are all leaves and flowers once more; the same sweet odor of mignonette floats up to my table as I write; everything around me is as charming as ever; all my dresses are most elegant; my poor last year's scarf, which you liked so much, is poked away out of sight, like everything else that is un-

worthy of the niece and heiress of Madame,
the Marchioness d'Aubecourt, and a soft
new one has taken its place; and as I am
very much to be envied, and consequently, I
suppose very happy. . . . Oh! why
should I hide from you that my grandeur
wearies and disturbs me, and that I am
wishing to be a little lower and to be happy
and at peace? Do not blame me, darling;
I am not moody, or restless, or melancholy;
I do try to be good, and even my castle-
building I am giving up, under the guidance
of the strict confessor to whom you brought
me. My books, my studies, my meditations
are all wise and well-chosen. There is only
one little breach by which restlessness steals
into my soul. You know my aunt, and you
know how she loves the world. She is always
running after it and dragging me with her;
and always bringing to her house crowds of
people whom I cannot care about. Years
do not make the slighest change in her.
She is always tender and affectionate, but
perhaps more than ever enamored of high-
sounding names and titles, etc.; and on this
point we shall always, always disagree,

though I try hard to hide it. She wants me to be always the niece and heiress of the Marchioness d'Aubecourt, and I know well enough that I am always, always, poor, simple Stephanie Corbin.

Now, this unfortunate Stephanie, being at the same time the niece and heiress of Mme. d'Aubecourt, is so rich a prize that she is continually contested for, much to the disturbance of her spirit. My aunt is highly amused thereat, but I cannot say I share her enjoyment. If they would only let me alone, or if there was the most remote chance of anyone turning up who would suit my ideas as well as my aunt's, I should not trouble my head about the matter; but, unhappily, this is most unlikely. My future husband —and it is continually impressed on me that I must soon make my choice—must of necessity conform to my aunt, and be a son to her as I am her adopted daughter. She has a set of ideas entirely different from mine; and, as she would naturally wish to give her affairs only into the hands of a person who would come up to these ideas, it follows as a natural consequence that she will, though without any desire to force my inclination, induce me to marry someone wholly unsuited to me. Every day I expect the commencement of a struggle between us on the subject—a struggle which I foresee will most probably end in my giving way out of sheer weariness and unwillingness to displease my aunt. It is not that I care for anyone myself; but I know that there is not one suited to me amongst all the elegant, eligible, well-born gentlemen, with a fashionable amount of brains, and all that society could desire, from amongst whom my aunt could any day choose a husband for her heiress. There are a good number of these gentlemen; and putting personal vanity aside and looking only to the beauty of this stately Hotel d'Aubecourt, and to the fertility of Madame d'Aubecourt's lands in Touraine, and the breadth of her acres in Brittany, and the richness of her vineyard in Burgundy, I begin to feel that Stephanie Corbin is a person of no small importance. Only there is question of the use which is to be made of the rich treasure, and her views on the subject may not quite chime in with those of the Marchioness d'Aubecourt.

Dear me! it seems that it is a wonderful thing that I should want to find someone who should be provided with that small but useful article, a heart to give in exchange for my own, as well as a title to give in exchange for my wealth.

Failing such a one, there is the Viscount, Henry de Sauveterre, on whom my aunt looks with most kindly eyes. He is young, handsome, good—at least everyone says so. I give no opinion; but I believe that our dear old friend, M. de Tourmagne, does not altogether go with the general prejudice in favor of the viscount. M. de Tourmagne might be very useful to me in an emergency. He has immense influence with my aunt: and I do not know a better soul or a warmer heart. No wonder you love him.

II.

MAY 8th.

You were right in supposing that the greater part of my last letter was dictated by thoughts which I did not fully unfold to you, dear Elise; and the truth was, that I

had not as yet dared to acknowledge them
even to myself. I was doing my best to
banish them as part of my imaginings and
black castle-building: for I do build black
castles as well as bright ones, great looming
things that rise up between me and the sunlight, until something happens to banish
them, or perhaps fix them as weary heart-
breaking truths—and this last is the case
this time, I fear. And now I shall tell you
all, for I may hold my tongue about my
dreams and foolish fancies but my real feelings and interests must not be hidden from
you; they are and always shall be yours.
Now, prepare that dear, wise head of yours
for a great weight of business; but for the
present speak to God only of what I am
going to say. Was ever anyone in so strange
a position as I am, or forced to act and think
in so strange a way? But I am twenty years
of age now; and I ask you, Elise, am I not
justified in taking the reins of my future
into my own hands, and refusing to sit by
tamely, and let all happiness, all brightness,
all goodness, drift away out of my life in a
forced marriage with one whose tastes, or

rather whose sympathies would be totally at variance with my own? If I must marry, as everyone seems determined I shall, and that soon, let it be someone worth marrying, worth loving and honoring. But where is such a person to be found? Not amongst the gentlemen I described in my last letter. And so I come to a subject which had made its way into my mind before I wrote to you, but which, as I said I had not dared to acknowledge to myself, and which now I dare breathe only to you and to God.

About a hundred steps from this palace of ours is a quiet old house, and there lives a man who, twelve years ago, almost saved my life, and who was more to me than the best of brothers. Neither my aunt nor any of her friends know anything about him; he passes me by without remembering me; but I remember, and if God helps me I will repay. I have reason to know that he is exactly what he was in those old days— pious, charitable, full of life, intelligence, and noble-heartedness; I owe him my life and more than my life; and, tell me, would it be wrong to work for his good and to

hope one day, by my love and gratitude, to
pay back the debt I owe? Having come so
far, everything seems at a standstill; it
seems impossible to go any further, and yet
I am not discouraged. I am in a very, very
strange position; I am literally at bay; the
thing is worth a trial, as I think you will
see when I tell you more about it. You can
be very useful to me in a thousand ways,
which I shall tell you of as we go along.
Now, dear, you have the groundwork of my
plan, and I cannot think you will find anything in it to offend either your reason or
your sense of right.

Meantime, M. de Sauveterre becomes
alarming. His attentions are redoubled,
and, my dear Elise, he has taken to sighing.
My aunt likes him and encourages him.
Does she reflect that she is in high favor
with the Dauphiness, and that one of our
friends, with whom she has very great influence, is a close friend of the favorite minister? M. de Sauveterre is a charming,
disinterested fellow, I am sure, and, of
course, never takes into consideration anything beyond the qualities and graces which

I possess—oh, dear, no! his ardor would be as great if I were a shepherdess. He insinuates as much, and why should I doubt him? Ah! my Lord de Sauveterre, is there not a golden halo round the head of the Marchioness d'Aubecourt's heiress which the head of the shepherdess would sadly lack? Even so, his lady mother, who, I fancy, has certain little hopes of becoming a peeress, is quite fit to calculate for the two. She is without exception the haughtiest, most arrogant countess I ever met. She is a Caniac, bear in mind, a Caniac of Perigord, not of Limousin—a fact which does not fail to dazzle my aunt a little, for the Caniacs of Limousin were, I hear, merely descendants of Abel, whilst the Caniacs of Perigord descended from Adam by primogeniture, or who knows, but they may even proceed from some man anterior to Adam, whom Moses passes over in silence. Her overweening pride of birth clings round her even in the *salon* of Mme. d'Aubecourt; and yet, only yesterday, in that very *salon*, I saw her labor almost obsequiously to repair a blunder of the viscount's, the utter foppish-

ness of which had appeared displeasing to
your insignificant friend, Stephanie Corbin,
daughter of a poor captain, grand-daughter
of a poor lawyer, great grand-daughter of
dear knows who, and dependent for some
time on the charity of a certain kind boy,
name unknown. But Stephanie's aunt is
rich, and in favor at court; and is it not
lawful to embrace meanness, if the alliance
is calculated to throw the ermine of the
peerage across the shield of the De Sauveterres? Ay, but I have my pride, too, and
it blazes out very fiercely sometimes, and
the more they fawn on me the more odious
they become. My interior insurrections are
not a little encouraged by the caustic remarks of M. de Tourmagne; he sees the
play of Mme. d'Aubecourt, and he does not
spare the charming viscount in his little
sarcasms.

Speaking of M. de Tourmagne, you will
be glad to hear that he has lately obtained
something he was wishing for very much.
He has been received into the *"Union"*
(mark this!), a member of the Academy
of Inscriptions. This is a very important

society of learned men who spend their time
in deciphering inscriptions written in the
half-effaced characters of half-forgotten lan-
guages on the ruined monuments of by-
gone people and bygone days. Anything
less than three thousand years old, M. de
Tourmagne looks upon as new, and hardly
worth counting. Perhaps this is why he
thinks so little of his own nobility, equal,
nevertheless, in antiquity even to that of the
Caniacs of Perigord.

III.

MAY 14th.

Since, with your never-failing friendship,
my own dear Elise, you have taken everything I have said at its best and found no
fault with all I have unfolded to you, though
I confess I was myself startled at first by the
very strangeness of my thoughts, I shall go
on to tell you what I have done, and how far
I have succeeded; but first you must have
the history of my life, which will place my
thoughts, my reasons, my position before you
in their true light. You little guess how

thickly sorrows and trials had lain on my
young life before I met you first in our
beloved Visitation Convent, and you must
come back a good way with me, for the knot
of my destiny was tied in tears and blood,
even before I had seen the light.

Towards the end of the Reign of Terror,
my grandfather, M. Raymond Corbin, late
lawyer of the Parliament of Poitou, was,
in two short awful days, arrested, brought
before the revolutionary tribunal of Laval,
accused of harboring priests and nobles,
found guilty, and condemned to death. The
poor old man trembled in his dark prison
as he thought of his old wife, so totally un-
provided for, of his fair daughter Valentine,
just grown up, and his brave younger son,
a fine young fellow of twenty, whom he had
lately observed, with sorrow, turning fast to
the new ideas. Three years ago his eldest
son had joined the army, and was most
probably a prisoner. And to all these was
added his crowning sorrow, that he must
die without the sacraments. In the midst
of these sad thoughts his prison door opened,
and a woman came in, followed by a poor

peasant, whose wandering eye and open
mouth spoke idiotcy in every line. The
woman was a Mademoiselle Joyant, a woman
before whose glorious charity the soldiers of
Laval used, strangely enough, to bend even
in their worst days. She was allowed to go
from prison to prison, attended by the poor
idiot, who helped her to distribute the good
things she brought with her. From her my
grandfather learned that his wife had also
been arrested, and his son obliged to go off on
an expedition against the Vendéens; but that
his daughter was safe, and in good hands.
Then, to his intense joy, she told him that
her companion was no idiot peasant, but a
disguised priest, who would give him the
last sacraments and prepare him for his
death on the morrow. Surely, my grandfather felt that night how God equals our
consolations to our afflictions. He charged
Mme. Joyant to bid his children adieu for
him, and to tell them how he blessed them.
"As for my dear noble wife," he added, "I
need send her no message. I know her, and
I know that she will be glad to die." The
scene had lasted some minutes; the gaolers

were getting impatient; and, pressing his hand, the brave woman passed out, with tears heavy in her eyes, and behind her went the priest with the poor, vacant face which he had enforced upon himself that he might devote himself to his sad, laborious duty. Three days passed before they came to lead M. Corbin to execution. He knew the reason of the delay when he saw his beloved wife seated in the cart which was to take them to the scaffold. The wretches had calculated on adding to the anguish of their victims by forcing them to suffer in each other's presence; but they only succeeded in giving them the greatest consolation. They had loved one another truly and devotedly, and they now remembered how in their happy days they had often told one another that they would love to die on the same day. They did die on the same day, at the same instant, and together rose the last prayers from their dying lips.

Mme. Joyant took Valentine under her care; but every day she prayed God to send the young girl some surer protection than she could give, for every day she expected to pay the penalty of her audacious piety.

One evening came the young Marquis Sylvester d'Aubecourt, a gentleman whom M. Raymond Corbin had sheltered a short time ago, disguised as a laborer. Valentine knew why he had come back so soon, and that gratitude was not the only feeling he had taken away with him. That night, in a little subterranean chamber, where many a hunted outcast had found safety during the past year, they were married by the very priest who had prepared M. and Mme. Corbin for death, whilst overhead sounded the trampling feet of the soldiers of Laval, making a search in the house. As their footsteps died away, the bride and bridegroom fled. At first all went well, and they were beginning to congratulate themselves on their good fortune, when they suddenly came on a station of Republican soldiers, and were stopped and questioned. In his anxiety for Valentine, the marquis, generally so brave, lost his presence of mind, stammered, and answered maladroitly. A sergeant who had lived in Laval declared Valentine to be the daughter of an aristocrat; and some wretches called *marsellais,*

who were of the very scum of the revolu-
tionaries, and who happened to be amongst
the soldiers, cried out that they should shoot
the man at once, and next day take the
daughter of the aristocrat to prison. The
marquis looked around him and shuddered.
The station was a lonely one, and could not
be relieved until morning. The full horror
of the situation burst upon him, and he
mentally determined, that if the worst came
to the worst, he would rather kill his inno-
cent wife with the poignard he had hidden
in his dress than leave her a night alone in
their hands. Luckily, some of the soldiers
took pity on them, and suggested that the
officer should be sent for. A discussion
ensued which gained time, and before it
was over the officer galloped up, having
been warned of the state of affairs by a boy
who had been watching the scene with terror and disgust. Valentine looked up at the
officer and recognized her younger brother.
With an instinct of their own peril and his,
neither of the fugitives gave the slightest
sign of joy or recognition, but left their
deliverance in his hands. Poor fellow!

what must have been his feelings when he saw whom he had to deal with. Though, like his elder brother, he inclined to the new ideas, he had the greatest respect for the Marquis d'Aubecourt, and he was devotedly attached to his sister Valentine. Perhaps the hope of being useful to her in the dangers that surrounded her had influenced him more than anything else in remaining with the revolutionary party. Now, he saw at a glance that their safety was in his hands. It might cost him his life to befriend them; but what generous heart would shrink from the thought of death at such a moment? Feigning to recognize the marquis as a workman whom he had often employed, he asked him where he was going, and who was the girl he had with him. "I am going to look for work at the manufactory of arms at Nantes," answered Sylvester, "and the girl is my wife. I found her completely alone in the world; I loved her, and I married her."

"Alone in the world?" echoed the officer, trying bravely to hide the sharp ring of pain in his voice. "Why, had she no father, or mother, or brother?"

"No," was the answer, "her father and mother are dead, and her two brothers are in the Republican service; but I hope to make up to her for all her losses."

"That will do," said the officer, "come with me and you shall have some supper, and then you may start once more on your journey."

They followed him as he rode silently before them through the dark night. Once he found means to slip some money into Sylvester's hand, and once he galloped round to his sister's side, and asked a short question to which she answered in a hurried whisper: "On the scaffold, blessing us with their last breath." And without daring to call them aside, without even touching their hands, he sent them away.

In a few days M. d'Aubecourt and his wife landed in England, and almost immediately afterwards they heard of their brother's death. One of his soldiers, since passed to the Catholic army, told them that Lieutenant Corbin had been denounced by his sergeant and shot. He fell, making the sign of the cross, and when some of his friends bent over him to receive his last breath, and to bear away his body, they heard him whisper the name of Jesus. It seemed as if the dying father had brought the revival of his son's faith, and the grace of a noble, glorious death. All these sad things, dear Elise, will help you to understand one strong trait in the character of my aunt, the much-tried Valentine Corbin, now widow of the Marquis d'Aubecourt—a trait which threatens in its strength to wield a very important influence in the disposition of my future. Her strongest feeling is an inveterate hatred and horror of the Revolution, of the ideas of the Revolution; nay, of anyone, or anything that she could suspect of being, or of ever having been, or of being ever likely to become in the slightest degree revolutionary. Whilst it is impossible to avoid seeing how truly good she is, how honorable in every little point, how gentle to everyone about her, and how humble before God, it is yet equally impossible to avoid seeing that she is unquestionably worldly. Her worship of the aristocratic equals in intensity her hatred of the revolutionary: a prejudice which, though she would not acknowledge it, she extends to all the *tiers état*. It is most evident; a plebeian name is positively hurtful to her ear, and seems at once to prejudice her against its unfortunate bearer; whilst a noble name, a noble title, seems to her to endow its possessor with all the beautiful qualities and virtues which she enjoyed in her husband, and her husband's friends. She forgets how brilliantly these very qualities shone in her own most *roturiére* family. She seems to hide and to ignore the fact that she was born a Corbin, and she is D'Aubecourt through and through, more thoroughly D'Aubecourt, I think, than any other D'Aubecourt that ever was born; so that I wonder that she ever forgave me for being my father's daughter; and I admire her for that forgiveness, even though it was tardy in coming.

IV.

MAY 15th.

My father was that eldest son of M. Raymond Corbin, who, as I told you, flew to arms at the first news of war, and who was sup-

posed to be a prisoner, or perhaps dead. He
had a generous, but a proud and indomitable
spirit, and having, it is believed, suffered
injustices, or perhaps injuries, from some
powerful persons just before the troubles
burst out, he conceived a haughty, undying
feeling of resentment, and became from that
moment as hot a revolutionary as my aunt,
later on, became a royalist. The cruelties
and villainies of the executioners of France,
though they horrified him, never caused him
to relinquish in the slightest degree his
fierce hatred of the past *régime*. He was
republican like the republicans of Rome,
thinking his soldier's work a hero's work,
and only longing to die on the battle-field,
a martyr to the cause which, though men
had dishonored, he believed to be just and
glorious before God. Even the death of his
father and mother, of which he heard as he
lay in his German prison, did not shake him.
My aunt sent him the particulars later on.
She had never spared his opinions; and her
letter and her news only plunged him deeper
into savage, moody despair; and he only
felt that he had no one in the world to care
for, and that he was weary of his life.

It was at this time that he met my mother. She was the daughter of a poor professor, a good man and a great philosopher, who partook of the feelings of the prisoner, became attached to him, and asked him to his home, the brightness and happiness of which was his only daughter. My father had a face like his spirit, noble, passionate, brave; and she was as pretty as she was gentle and good. They soon came to love one another; and for the first time for many weary years a ray of light stole into the grief-stained heart of the stern soldier. It was a sad joy to both. Two such hearts might love one another more than life, but not more than duty; and each tried to hide the secret that the other saw; for they were poor. Oh! Elise, Elise, how many a heart is wrung and thrown back upon itself by that cold, stern hand of Poverty! How many warm, beautiful, passionate hearts cry out to one another, longing to share together the sufferings that would be only links to bind them closer, the joys that were only joys by union; but Mammon comes, and with proud, scornful smile flings them asunder to beat out all softness, all sweetness—alone in the struggle. He longed to give his darling the strong support of his brave heart, and her true heart beat to think how she might console him with her sweet devotion; but the woman shrank back proudly from daring to tempt the duty that her beloved owed his country; and the man bowed calmly before the brave girl, whose first duty lay with her aged father. And only sweet, pure Duty flung her moonlight across the sad, dark face of Poverty. Only God could aid them. The old philosopher was— though such examples were at that time rare in Germany—a fervent Catholic. His daughter had followed in his footsteps; and now her enthusiastic heart was full of the desire to awaken in her lover's heart ere their separation the ardent piety which had power to calm the storms in her own. She succeeded. My father had rather forgotten than relinquished the faith of his early years, and at her loved touch it shone out the brighter for the very strength of his misfortunes. You know, dear Elise, how tenderly we come to love God when He calls us to Him through sorrow.

Soon came the news of peace and the order for surrender of prisoners. The two sad hearts were preparing to say their last adieu, when something happened which changed the whole face of their destiny. The old professor died suddenly, having only time to beg his friend to take care of his beloved daughter. So my father took his precious legacy, and a year afterwards I was born. I think that my birth was about the last joy that he tasted. This was in 1800. My father had left the army; for he would not serve the ambition of Buonaparte, which was as distasteful to him as the infamies of the Revolution; and he threw away his sword and began to work. But the very honesty which prompted him to this course exposed him to dangers to which, in his inexperience, he succumbed. He was informed against amongst the men connected with the Government. The noble audacity of his language drew down a persecution which wrought his ruin, and brought him face to face with utter misery. Years of awful struggle passed, years of fearful trials, and left him crushed and broken-hearted,

but still full of courage, on the very
threshold of death, with his wife and little
daughter, seven years old, totally unpro-
vided for.

You will probably ask why he did not
write to his sister, the Marchioness d'Aubecourt, in such a strait as this. Ah! Elise,
this is one of the saddest things I have to
tell, though my aunt's fault was excusable,
considering how little she knew of his neces-
sities and the views she held; and since then
how she has labored to atone! My father's
letter was, most probably, too proud; and
my poor aunt answered quickly with one
equally so. She had the imprudence to rake
up his unfortunate opinions, and to show
herself the ardent royalist when she should
have been, as she was in truth, only the
loving sister. Smarting under their misfortunes, and the more sensitive because they
had suffered so intensely, my father and
mother bitterly and scornfully refused the
help which would have saved them. My
aunt, in her turn, offended, and besides,
ignorant of the extent of their need, did not
insist. Afterwards her generous heart re-

gretted it all, and she took steps to find her
brother, which were unfortunately ineffec-
tual. He had disappeared, taking cruel care
to hide his whereabouts and even his name;
and my mother, as haughty as he, prevented
nothing, but quietly followed him to the
wretched lodging where he stoically endured
his slow martyrdom. Oh! Elise, the picture
of that horrible garret is always before my
eyes. It was in one of the blackest houses
in the most miserable part of the town, and
it is always associated in my mind with sorrow and wretchedness. They sent me to a
little school and kept me there for some time
with the price of the last remnants of our
poor furniture. Then came a day when my
mother knelt in the dark, ugly room, pale
and agonized, but with calm, dry eyes, holding on her bosom the dying head of the husband who had been her first love, and whose
every look had been her support in their
stormy life of sorrow. His hands were
joined and his eyes fixed on a crucifix
whilst he listened to the words of a priest
standing at the foot of his bed. This is
what my awe-stricken little eyes saw as the

door opened. He smiled when I stole in,
and then kissed me lovingly, and I knelt
down, so that he could lay his hand on my
bowed head. Then he said: "My little
daughter, you shall never see me in this
world again. Pray for me; take care of
your dear, dear mother, and put all your
confidence in the good God who is comfort-
ing me so much to-day, though I am leaving
you. Never hesitate when there is a duty
to be done; be always a follower of our
Lord; and now God bless you, my little
child, in the name of the Father, and of the
Son, and of the Holy Ghost."

Then they took me away, Elise, and he
died that night.

V.

MAY 16th.

When my brave mother had followed her
idolized husband to the grave, and she had
nothing but me left, she turned, and taking
her courage in both hands, made up her
mind to live and work for me. She was
robust and industrious, and she contrived

for two or three months, at the cost of God
knows what fatigues and privations, to pay
my little school fee. After that she suddenly found herself penniless. She had to
take me away; hunger stared us in the face,
and it seemed as if we must leave even that
wretched home. At this point the mother's
love triumphed over her pride, and she made
up her mind to beg help from Mme. d'Aubecourt. She took steps to find out where
she lived, and was about to write to her
when God sent us another friend.

One morning a young man walked in, a
tall, slight young man, with a calm, brave
face, who said that a Sister of Charity had
told him of our distress, and sent him to
help us. I do not know all he said that
morning in the dark garret, but I know that
he brought happiness with him, and that he
threw brightness across our lives, like the
long streak of sunlight that came in with
him through the open door, and lay all along
the ground to our feet. When he was gone,
promising to come back, my mother fell on
her knees with the grateful tears welling up
in her sad eyes and running down her poor,

pale face. Then, I remember, she dressed me and took me out to a neighboring church, and she prayed very long; and when I had said my *Hail Marys* I sat with my crossed feet swinging backwards and forwards, watching how the sun shone through a bright window where St. Raphael was pictured going in human form to help the young Tobias, and how the beautiful colors lay in splatches on the white floor. Then I thought a great deal about our new friend, and he got mixed up in my mind with the bright, sunny, kind St. Raphael; and to this day he is vividly associated in my mind with the beauty and brightness of that church, where the morning sun poured in through the painted window, and with the charity of the sweet St. Raphael: perhaps there was some look in his face like that of the picture. At last my mother rose, and we went out and bought some food with the money he had given us. When we came back, and I sat eating my bread, my mother threw her arms around me and kissed me, saying: "My poor little one, we are not alone in the world, and father is praying for us." No wonder that day made a never-to-be-forgotten impression upon my mind and heart.

Next day he came again with more good news. He had made arrangements, and very probably paid also, for my reception into an orphanage, and he was to take me there immediately. Then came plans for my mother. She was very accomplished, and could paint flowers beautifully. He would get her pupils, and meantime she must have a little money, just a loan, he said, that she might be a little better dressed and lodged before the pupils came. His exquisite tact made it a real pleasure to accept his bounty. It grieved him, he said, to have us thank him; for he was only the agent of some very rich, charitable people who employed him in their hidden good works. And then how delightful it was when, to crown all, my mother discovered that he had lived in Germany, and could speak her beloved native language; and truly happy days succeeded to all our misery. In my convent I was a great pet; and every week my mother and our friend came to see me, he always bring-ing me some little present. I have a beautiful rosary which he gave me there treasured up as a very precious thing. Meantime, thanks to him, pupils began to come to my mother's house, and she soon enjoyed what seemed to be ease in comparison to our former pinching poverty.

One Sunday morning M. Germain (that was the only name by which I knew him) came very early to take me, he said, to see a certain lady who was very fond of me.

It seemed to me that we went through the whole of Paris, with the bright sun peeping up the streets and over the houses at us, and the soft morning air fanning our faces as we walked along, I clinging to M. Germain's hand and chatting merrily. At last we stopped at a nice comfortable-looking house, and went up a bright staircase; then a door opened, and I was in my mother's arms in a pretty room;—oh! so different from the hideous garret I had left. A room with fresh, pretty furniture, and fair, white curtains hanging round a large window which opened on a vista of greenness and sunshine. Birds were hopping about, and chirping in the branches of the trees that waved up

close under the window, and a sweet, balmy,
flowery smell came floating in. I hopped
about like one of the little chatterers outside, crying: "Oh! mamma, mamma, how
pretty! how nice and comfortable you are
here!"

She watched me with moistened eyes,
whispering: "It is all M. Germain's doing,
dear; all M. Germain's doing."

"No," he said, in the same low tone, "not
my doing."

Almost instinctively our eyes followed his
to the crucifix on which my father had fixed
his dying looks. He lifted me up in his
arms and carried me over, that I might kiss
the feet of my real Benefactor. I could go
on, and on, giving you every little detail of
that day, for every moment of it is engraved
on my mind. With the exception of my
First Communion Day I remember no other
in all my life so utterly happy. We all
went to Mass together, and then we came
back to breakfast, and chatted away in my
mother's beloved German like three very
happy people, as we were. I suppose it was
some vague impression of our extreme hap-

piness in being united in this way that entered into my little heart when I suddenly looked up and said in a very serious tone: "Mother, when I am big, I will marry Germain!"

"What!" she said, half vexed and half amused.

But Germain laughed, and asked, "Why not?"

"Well," I explained, nothing abashed, "I love him so much, and I cannot be his sister, because he is not your son."

"Well, look here, Rœschen"—(Stephanie is not my real name, though my aunt has called me so; Rœschen or Rosalie, is the name I was christened)—"look here, Rœschen," replied my bridegroom-elect, "you must first of all be my sister, because we are two of God's children; and then, later on, if you are wise, and good, and learn to sew and to count, we shall see about the rest."

Bear this in mind, Madame Elise, and hold yourself ready, when the time comes, to bear testimony to the fact that I am perfect mistress of the four rules, and am generally considered passing deft and cunning with my needle; for I have some idea of holding M. Germain to his old engagement.

This happy time stretched itself over about two bright years. My mother began to be able to meet my little pension as it came due, and even gradually to pay back the money which Germain had lent her. He very often came to see me, always the same, always kind, and gentle, and good. And now and then we had one of those happy little reunions. He was more like a relation to us than merely our benefactor and friend. He used to say himself that in our big, lonely Paris we stood him instead of his absent mother and sister. For my part, I loved him as dearly as ever I could love any brother. Many a time, when he was taking me back to the convent in the evening, after one of those grand days, I would fall asleep in the carriage, with my head against his shoulder, and his arm around me to keep me up; and in winter he would roll me tenderly in his warm, soft cloak, just as if I was indeed his dear little sister.

One sad day he came and told us that his studies would oblige him to make a long

journey, and that he was come to bid us
good-bye. We did not want his help now,
but, Elise, we did want his love and friendship. How I cried and sobbed that day;
my mother kept me at home and tried to
console me, telling me that he would come
back again after his tour and be always with
us. But I felt as if I had lost my second
father, and cried on inconsolably for my
dear, dear Germain. A great grief, however, soon threw this one far in the shade.
About five or six months after Germain's
departure my mother fell ill. She had
drooped slowly since my father's death; her
spirit alone had kept up her shattered
health; toil, and anxiety, and care about
my future had gradually, gradually dried
up the very sap of her existence. Now she
felt that her hour was come; and putting
aside hesitation and fear of humiliation or
refusal, she gathered up her dying courage,
for love of her child, and wrote to Madame
the Marchioness d'Aubecourt. My aunt,
who had been some years a widow, was not
in Paris; she was at that beautiful place in
Brittany where we have spent so many

happy vacations together. This time her answer was worthy of herself; the generous heart of old Raymond Corbin's daughter spoke, and spoke alone. She travelled day and night, and never rested until she reached our door. She was just in time. My dear mother, speechless and dying, had only sufficient strength left to embrace her sister-in-law and to point to her little weeping daughter. Next day she died with the serenity of an angel as she was; and my aunt, having stayed some days in Paris, and seen to all the last wants, carried me off to Brittany.

As a first piece of advice, delivered amidst a shower of caresses, which won their way straight to my lonely little heart, she told me that she would rather I did not speak of my father or mother, or of the past at all, to anyone but herself. Child as I was, I soon began to see that it would be better to avoid these subjects with her as well as with everyone else; and, little by little, our sorrows and our joys, the dark, poor attic, the little convent, the pretty room, with the white curtains and the waving trees outside, even my dear, dear Germain and all his goodness, faded away and sank into the gloom of by-gone remembrances. Even my own identity seemed to grow dim. I was not Rœschen now, or Rosalie; for that name seemed un-accountably to displease my aunt (perhaps some servant had borne it); and I became rich Stephanie and quite another person from that poor little girl that I knew of old. The metamorphosis was completed on that day when I was taken to the Visitation Convent, and when you also arrived there, dearest. How little you dreamt what sad, sad shadows had fallen across the young life of your favorite companion, the merry, petted niece of the rich and good Marchioness d'Aubecourt.

I stayed there, as you know, until I was sixteen years of age, and I would have stayed there always if my aunt had seemed in the least to desire it. Not that I felt that I had a decided vocation, not that I dreaded the sorrows and dangers of the world; but it seemed to me that in the cloister, so safely shut in, bound to heaven by eternal vows, and going daily through that round of hum-

ble work, falling so lightly on the shoulders
of innocence and prayer, the spirit might
find the surest, and, perhaps, the only true
good of life, which my soul has always pursued with outstretched arms—peace. Eight
years of my new life had gone by, and only
a very vague remembrance remained of the
woes of my childhood. Their sad figures
flitted by less and less distinctly as time went
on, until they grew almost sweet; and yet,
in Madame d'Aubecourt's presence they
would rise up, bringing with them a feeling
that weighed on my conscience like a sense
of ingratitude. They clung around me in
my aunt's superb mansion, pointing to the
luxury around me and whispering that the
price of even one of those costly objects
would have bought my father's life, until
my thoughts seemed to become accusations
against my adopted mother.

It was as if a cloud, a light, rapid cloud,
floated across my real gratitude; but to
escape that cloud I would, or at least I
thought I would, willingly enter the convent. "But then," I argued, "perhaps in
the world I may meet M. Germain again.

How I should thank him! What talks we should have about my mother! It would be like having herself back with me again!"

And then my heart would beat very quickly and my project would seem farther away from my heart than ever.

My aunt herself put an end to these doubts. She came to take me away from the convent, folding me in her arms, and telling me that I was her darling, and should be her sole heiress. I was far more touched by her tenderness than by her rich promises. She had only me in the world, she said, and I should be the happiness of her old days. Of those two families which had flourished for thirty years, we, in truth, were the only ones left. Death had struck at the proud trunk of the D'Aubecourts as well as the humble stem of the Corbins, and left only us two. Should we not be all in all to each other?

Besides, my aunt is so good. It was from her that I heard my father's history up to the time when he appealed to her for help, and when, as she generously acknowledged, she repulsed him. Hundreds of times I have

seen the tears in her eyes as she thought of
it; and yet, strange as it may seem, I feel
that, whilst she does justice to her brother's
noble heart, she never pardons him for
having been a *jacobin*, though, for my sake,
she refrains from giving him the objection-
able name, and contents herself with bitterly bewailing his political errors. Of the
rest of our adventures she has only a very
general idea, and evidently does not wish
to be further enlightened; so that I have
always, first through instinct, and then
through charity, refrained from speaking
much about them. Once, a long time ago,
I ventured on something about a certain
young gentleman who had been such a
benefactor to my mother and myself, but
she interrupted me so hastily, and with
such a troubled face, that Germain's name
died away on my lips unspoken. This, of
course, was most excusable. It must naturally be very bitter to her to think that anyone in the world could have it in his power
to say: "I gave alms to the sister-in-law
and niece of the Marchioness d'Aubecourt;
I drew them out of misery when she had

cast them there." For she does not know
Germain's character, and she might form a
strange idea about him. But I know him,
or I am very much deceived. He has re-
appeared; I have seen him; I know where
he lives. But I dare not say to Mme. d'Aubecourt: "The man who helped and saved
my mother's life and my own, is living a
few steps away from your house; perhaps
you could be of use to him." With all her
generosity, I fear she would not offer Germain what I would wish to give him.

VL

MAY 20th.

I have not, as you say, dear Elise, as yet
told you how I discovered our old friend;
but now you shall have the whole story. It
was almost immediately after I left the Visitation that my aunt first spoke to me on the
subject of marriage. I saw that she wished
me to marry early. I also saw that she
would expect me to make my choice from
amongst the gentlemen I have already described to you, and this I was determined

I would never do without a struggle. Then it was that I thought of my old hero, the truest, bravest man I had ever known; and I formed the strange plan of attempting to find him by that one solitary clue, his name —Christian name or surname, I knew not which—Germain. The first place I turned to was the orphanage where I had been to school, and which, I remembered, was in a faubourg behind the *Jardin des Plantes;* thinking it just possible that Germain might have kept up some sort of connection with it. I found the street, but not the convent; and on going to the house of the Curé of the parish, I found a young priest instead of the old man I had left. He told me that the religious had given up the convent some years ago, and were now scattered amongst different houses of their congregation.

"Is there one of these houses in Paris?" I asked.

"No," was the answer.

"And where is the mother house?"

"In Languedoc."

Move number one unsuccessful. Now for move number two. I had always kept my

mother's address, which was a place at the
other side of Paris, and I went straight
there. I discovered the house, entered with
a beating heart, and found myself face to
face with the old porter of our own days.

"Did you know Madame Corbin who
lived here once?" I asked.

"Yes, Mademoiselle, but she is dead these
ten years," was the reply.

"And her daughter?" came next.

"The daughter is gone back to Germany."

"To Germany?" I echoed.

"Yes; with some of her rich relations."

The reply actually froze me. It showed
how anxious Madame d'Aubecourt must
have been to blot me out from the memory
of those who had known us in our misfortunes. She had striven, as it were, to bury
Rœschen in her mother's grave, and to give
to Stephanie a new life which she should
hold from her.

"And has no one ever come to ask for
Madame Corbin or her daughter?" I asked,
opening my purse and letting a piece of gold
shine before his eyes.

"It is really so long ago, Mademoiselle,"

answered the man, "that I do not remember.
I know that Madame Corbin's friend paid
everything like a princess, and ordered that
her clothes and furniture should be given
to the poor."

"No letters belonging to her remain, I
suppose?" I asked, as a sort of forlorn hope.

"Oh! wait a moment," he cried, as if
struck with a new idea. He turned and
called to his wife: "Isn't there a letter there
for a lady who is dead?"

"I think so—what name?"

"Madame Corbin," I answered, trembling.

She poked about for awhile in a drawer
full of old papers and rags, and at last drew
out a letter, very much crushed and very
yellow, and read:

"Madame—Madame Corbin, painter of
flowers;" and, with a low "that's it," I held
out my trembling hand. The porter took
my gold, and gave me my prize. It was
from Italy, and, though I did not know the
writing, I guessed it was from Germain. In
my own room that night with locked door,
I drew out my letter and prepared to read
it, feeling that I was going to raise the

curtain that hung over my knowledge of
these two dear ones, and that some great
new phase of my life was opening before me.
For one moment a scruple crossed my mind,
of whether I had a right to read what was
meant for my mother's eye alone. I said a
little prayer, and then, feeling as if she herself was bidding me do it, I broke the seal.
I looked first at the signature, Germain *D*.
That told me nothing. Must even Germain's own letter hide his name from me?
It could not hide his character, however;
that, at least, I learned and I want you to
know it also. I send you a copy of his letter.

GERMAIN'S LETTER TO MY MOTHER.

"NAPLES, November 21st, 1811.

"MY DEAR FRIEND,

"To-morrow I start for Smyrna, where I
expect to stay some time and to make out a
regular route for my wanderings, and so I
write to bid you good-bye. You speak to
me of gratitude, but it is I who have real
cause to be grateful. Little do you know
how much the sight of your brave goodness

has done for me. It was a blessing of God that I was allowed to be of use to you; and in assisting you I enjoyed a sweet and useful recreation, which never hindered my studies, and from which I always came back better and 'refreshed. During these last three months that I have been at home I have spoken of you very often. My mother sees, as I do, the beneficial effect your influence has had upon my character; and little Jeanne is ready to love Rœschen as her own sister. If I had given up the idea of travelling, they would have come to live with me in Paris, and then my mother would have been a true friend to you, and like a second mother of Rœschen; which consideration, I assure you, made me waver a little; but my determination got the upper hand. I must travel; I must see the great world, expand my mind, and be a man, and, I hope, a learned man. How I thank my mother now that she dissuaded me from becoming a soldier. The hardships of military service are now far less distasteful to me than are the waving plumes, the glittering swords, and all the gay appendages of military glory

that dazzled my boyish eyes of old. I would
rather be the most humble of philosophers
than the most brilliant of hussars; I would
rather discover the date of a town than gain
a victory; I would rather win the chair of a
librarian than the baton of a marshal. I
will never base my fortune on the blood and
ruin of others; I will think for myself, act
for myself, follow my own sweet will, not
like those automatons who work under the
control of one man against their kind.
These thoughts were in my heart when
I met you; they had come down to me
from my father; but they lay dormant.
Your words, your observations, your ideas
awakened them and fixed them for ever. I
can never thank you enough. My opinions
have expanded and shaped themselves since
then, and now I think that only the gilded
dress of the republicans, and the traces
their reign has left behind it, restrain me
from very republican sentiments. And
behind the thought of their crimes and
monstrosities rises my ideal of liberty and
justice, which, perhaps, we shall never see,
but which is not the less beautiful, and by

the light of this ideal I see, in a very hatefu¹ aspect, all this administrative livery and military display in which we are first amongst the nations of the world. Then, my mother urges that it is quite possible, without being either soldier or coward, to remain in France, and even to become a professor or a philosopher. But, then, what is to become of the ardent desire I have always had, to see, to compare, to reason, to judge for myself? I could not settle down quietly in Paris without running the greatest risks, from that very love of adventure which once attracted me to the military life. In fact, all things considered, it is better for me to go. I am sure you will agree with me that three or four years of wanderings in these countries which have so strange an attraction for me, will be of far more use to me than ten spent in the libraries. I certainly love books, but they alone could never satisfy me. I want scope. And so, armed with my splendid health, away I go into the bold, free air, to follow the peregrinations of Theseus.

"You must never forget me in your prayers, dear friend, for I am bound for

countries where steeples are few. God alone
can tell how I shall act so far away for all
spiritual helps; and yet something tells me
that I shall never go astray. When I think
of the happiness of being a Christian in
such times as these, I feel my heart full of
proud security. I throw myself, with confidence equal to my love, into the arms of that
Immense Mercy which has protected me so
long and so powerfully; and you, of course,
may always count on my prayers such as
they are. I think we might almost take
these things for granted without telling
them to one another. As to Rœschen, my
other little sister, I must have her *Ave
Marias* following me as mine shall follow
her. Dear little Rœschen! You will be
a happy mother, dear Madame Corbin, if
Rœschen turns out all that I expect. There
is a mixture of strength, enthusiasm, and
intense feeling in her character that ought
to make her a splendid girl. You will see
that she will grow up pretty, too, with her
French eyes and her German hair. She has
a grand heart, brave as her father's and tender as yours—one of those hearts that seem

to be naturally preserved from unworthi-
ness, as if the beautiful and the good were
their natural element. Poor little thing!
God guard her from such trials as yours;
but those very sorrows have, I think, built
a sort of fortification round her little heart
that will benefit her in after life, as I
solemnly believe sorrow always does. I
should not wonder if she became a nun; it
would be a great happiness for her.　.　.　.
but suppose she does not become a nun; I
may as well tell you before I go away.
When I return after, say, five years of travel,
Rœschen will be almost marriageable, and I
have planned another life of happiness for
her. Of course we are both poor, but who
will make that objection? Not my mother
or you, and I am sure not Rœschen; and,
besides, with a little hard work, we should
have quite enough to live. Now, laugh at
my castles in the air as you please, it is a little castle that the ivy of my love is fast wrap-
ping round. My little wife will have been
brought up by you, and partly by myself;
and she has been accustomed to think of me
as someone to lean on and look up to. Of

course, we shall not force her heart; but do you remember how prettily she said one day: 'Mother, when I am big, I will marry Germain.' It will be very sweet for me to look forward, after all my wanderings, to come back and hide myself from the world, and rest in the peace of a happy home. I would like my wife to have known poverty, to be very pious, to have a pure soul, and a loving heart; I would like that before loving me as her husband she had loved me as a brother; I would have her whole heart, and life, and memory full of my image. Do not think me egotistical. I know I express myself badly, but indeed my feelings must be put down to something better; I know that my wife will have many faults to put up with in me, and I know that to do so easily she must love me: I know you will agree with me here, for you know me better than I know myself.

"I must now speak of business and bring this long letter to a close. You pretend that you owe me some money, and I am going to tell you how to get rid of it. Part of it is to be spent on Rœschen on the day of her First Communion. I *wish* (do not be vexed, this is the way to write a will), that she should get a grand wax taper and a handsome veil which will do her again on her wedding-day; the rest you may give to the poor after spending some on Masses for my intention. But all this is only on one condition with which I charge you on your honor. It is that the first time you want anything, as I told you before I left, you must go at once to M. N. whose address I gave you, and whom I have told about you. He has something in reserve which he can send you at once; and besides he is so generous and charitable, that he will be glad to be of service to you. Do not hesitate for a moment to send to him when you are in an emergency. Think of your daughter, and, may I say it, think of your friend.

"May our blessed Lady and the saints and angels protect you and bear to God's throne the earnest prayers I send up for you.

"GERMAIN D."

Put yourself in my place, Elise, and fancy how this letter made me feel. I sat with my hands folded across it, thinking what a character he must have, and feeling that dull pain at the heart which comes with a flood of regret for something we have longed for and lost. Every night for the next month I sat up for ever so long, reading it; I soon knew it by heart, and still I read it and read it. Whenever I got the chance, I was off to my room, and there I would draw out my treasure and pore over it, gazing silently at the signature as if I expected the mute initial sooner or later to give up its secret. That was all I could do at present, there was no step I could take in my search just now. I did not remember anything about the M. N. of whom Germain spoke, but most probably he had called to inquire for my mother and written the news of her death to his friend. Then came the thought that perhaps Germain himself was dead; there were many chances in favor of the supposition that he had lost his life in his long and dangerous journey. In my next conversation with M.

de Tourmagne I brought him round to the
subject of his travels in the East; but he
drew such frightful pictures that I interrupted him and ran away in a worse frame
of mind than ever. Once I had an idea of
telling everything to my aunt and giving
her Germain's letter, but my courage failed
me. At last she spoke to me of marriage;
and at the first word I burst out crying and
begged her to wait. I would give her no
explanation, but assured her that I did not
intend to become a nun. Certainly, I did
not. I had one of those strong, unconquer-
able presentiments that sometimes come to
us, that I should see Germain again. I had
no attraction to the religious life. I even
showed a sudden taste for the world which
astonished and delighted my aunt. I was
silly enough to hope that in some of these
most brilliant, and aristocratic, and elegant
assemblages I should meet Germain, my
poor, simple Germain. Of course I was disappointed, as we generally are when our
hopes take such absurd flights. When M.
de Tourmagne invited us to his house, I
went with the thought that, Germain being

a *savant,* I might find him there. I astonished our good friend every now and then
by dropping in and asking him to show me
some of his books about the East. He was
obliged to escort me about to all the libraries; and when I discovered that they had
an Academy of Science, he must take me
there also. But Germain was nowhere to
be seen, and I began to give up.

Then came a greater hatred than ever of
society. I was tired looking round brilliant
rooms to be disappointed, tired of feeling
that worst of loneliness, loneliness in a
crowd, tired of contrasting the insipid conversation of my fashionable admirers with
the true, grand spirit breathed in that dear
letter at home. Nothing would induce me
to stir out of doors, I would do nothing
but mope and fret. The doctors told my
startled aunt that I must have change of air
and scene. She asked me where I would
like to go; and I coaxed M. de Tourmagne,
who treated me as a spoiled child, to accom-
pany me to Italy. I wanted to breathe the
air of Naples.

You might have seen how well, and even gay, I seemed after that trip. The truth was, that I very wisely, but with a great effort of determination, left Germain's letter behind me here—that letter is a talisman that always throws me into dreamland. After a great deal of reasoning with myself, and after a great deal of prayer I conquered myself, and came back from Italy wiser and better. God gave me grace in those long hours of union with Him, my heart became quieter and I a more reasonable being. I certainly always held to the desire of seeing Germain again, and I know that I clung to him with some sort of vague hope; but, then, how often do we take our dearest hopes and wishes and lay them sadly away in some hidden chamber of our hearts, knowing that they lie there just as dear and sacred as ever, though we must give them up. Sometimes, I would take my letter in my hands and look at it for awhile, but I never let myself open it. I often said to myself: if I find that reason advises and my aunt's happiness demands that I should marry, I will take Germain's letter and burn

it without ever opening it again, but nothing
else can ever weaken or destroy the feelings
that have taken so strong a hold upon my
heart.

I had just reached this heroic but rather
gloomy height of determination, when I
wrote that letter to you three weeks ago, on
the subject of your marriage, which made
me look back so sadly at my own life, and a
few days after—I saw, Germain!

VII.

MAY 22d.

It was on Sunday, at Mass, in the Parish
Chapel, that I saw him. I was beside my
aunt, and we were turning towards the pulpit to listen to the sermon, when my eyes fell
upon Germain, right opposite us, and not
three steps away. I knew him at the very
first glance. He is grand, Elise. I am sure
you are dying to hear what he is like. He
looks grave and manly. The thick clusters
of hair on his forehead are beginning to thin
just a little, but except for that, the calm,
good face is not changed. His dress is very

simple, and yet there is something elegant about it. Anyone might feel proud to belong to him.

His head was turned towards the preacher, and so I had plenty of time to look at him. It is he, himself, I thought, the very Germain that I remembered, the very Germain that I pictured to myself. Then, I cast down my eyes again, I tried to draw down my veil, I shrank behind a very stout lady who happened to be between us, and began to think. I am afraid I did not hear much of the sermon that day; and, moreover, I am afraid I fell into a reverie, for I know I was troubled with very strong remembrances of a certain morning in a dark garret, and of a little child sitting on a bench behind her mother's kneeling figure, and St. Raphael with a kind, sweet face blazing out of a painted window overhead. Then, with a start, I came back to Stephanie, wondering what my dead mother would advise me to do now, what I ought to do, where my duty lay. When the sermon was over I fell on my knees, and burying my face in my hands implored God to grant that I might be the

wife of my mother's benefactor or remain
unmarried all my days. O Germain, Germain, I could not give away the heart that
was not mine to give, for it is as full of you
as you desired it to be!

My aunt rose to leave the church, and
I followed. We passed slowly by the bench
where Germain knelt, and I ventured to take
just one look at him. He was praying with
head bowed down, and a few gray hairs scattered among the locks about his temples told
me what a laboricus life he had been leading
since I saw him last. I recognized his prayer-
book for he taught me *to read Latin* in it, and
I wondered if there was a little picture of St.
Rose of Palermo there, which I had given
him shortly before our separation. My aunt
remarked him, and observed that he seemed
very pious. Why could I not say "I know
him. He is my benefactor, my oldest, truest
friend." However, that remark of her's
seemed a good omen as well as the fact that
it was in so holy a place that Providence had
allowed me to see my old friend again. Once
outside the church my first feeling was dread
that I should lose sight of him. I darted up

to my own room to watch which way he
would go. Presently from my post behind
the curtains I saw him pass down a very
quiet street just opposite the Hotel d'Aubecourt. He gave something to that poor old
woman whom you may remember to have
seen always there with her crucifix on her
breast and her *Ave Maria* on her lips.
Thanks to my long sight, I was able to
watch him all down the street till he entered a plain but pretty-looking house at the
end, which is shut in like a convent. By-
and-by he came out again, without his
prayer-book, so I concluded that it was his
own house. What a lot of discoveries all in
one day! To see him, to know that he was
alive and well, and to find him living just
within sight of my own window. He came
up the street and passed our house with an
attentive look at the carved escutcheoned
doorway and windows. Germain! Germain!
look again, don't pass by so quickly. Your
little Rœschen is watching you behind the
rich curtains of one of those sculptured windows that have caught your eye, and loving
you better than she did in those old, happy

days, even such a love as you wished her to
have for you. But without another thought
of the gorgeous Hotel d'Aubecourt, and still
less of poor Rœschen, he went on and soon
was out of sight. Then I rose with a great
sigh, locked the door, took out my precious
letter, unfolding it with a sort of tender respect and renewing in my heart the prayer I
had made an hour before in the presence of
God. At Vespers that evening he was in
the very same place, "so, most probably," I
thought, "he belonged to the parish, and I
shall see him very often." A fortnight went
by and I saw him every day. Nearly every
morning we met at Mass and then he disappeared into his quiet-looking old house and
did not come out again until evening, or
if he did pass the threshold he was back
directly with two or three awful-looking old
books tucked affectionately under his arm;
from all of which I concluded that he had
no particular occupation except study, and
that he was not changed since he wrote that
wonderful letter. Once or twice I saw him
at a particular window in which a light
burns until the most unearthly hours; and

this I supposed was his own room, and probably his study also. You will smile at all
this, I know, dear ; but my life is very sweet
just now. I piece out my little puzzle every
day. When I waken, I feel that he is not far
away. I guess at all his occupations as the
day goes on. I kneel near him in the church.
I pray for him, little as he suspects it ; and I
wait in hopes of some day having an opportunity of showing him what a grateful,
loving heart I have. Sometimes he looks sad
and careworn ; and I think that he has some
great trials to bear, and I long so much to
comfort him who comforted us in our troubles. He looks lonely too ; I wonder where
his mother and sister can be.

He does not recognize me in the least.
Sometimes he happens to glance at me in
passing ; but it does not seem to awaken the
slightest remembrance in his mind. You
know one sometimes see on peoples' faces
a look as if they were trying to remember
where they had seen you. Of course, I was
only ten years old when he went away and
now I am twenty, just double the age I was
then. Besides, at that time I was a misera-

ble and rather plain child, and now I am a
girl, and if the opinions of M. de Sauveterre
and his mother are to be relied upon, rather
a nice girl. Well, there is no use in my
hiding anything from you, Elise, and I do
not think you will be vexed with me for
what I am going to say. I wish that Monsieur Germain could hold the same opinion
on this subject as my aristocratic admirer.
But I laugh to see the two men side by side
in my mind, and to fancy two such different
beings having any feeling in common, and I
fear the contrast is hardly complimentary to
the Viscount de Sauveterre.

VIII.

MAY 27th.

No, Elise, I could not speak to my aunt
about him. The reasons which I have
already urged to you, and of which you
have taken no notice, seem to be insur-
mountable. Besides, there is the fear that,
if my aunt attempted to admit him as a *pro-
tégé* into her house, she would scare him
altogether. I also feel that if I ventured

even to pronounce his name, anyone could
read my secret in my face. Now, it does not
follow that because I wish to tell all to you,
because I feel a want to tell all to you, I
must necessarily tell everyone else. You
know the very depths of my heart and of
my character, and to you the singularity of
my situation accounts for all my thoughts,
and feelings, and desires. I loved Germain,
I may say, before I saw him, because of his
magnificent character. I love him ten times
as much now that I see him every day, and
every day see something new to admire in
him. I say it to you without a blush, for
while it is a secret between us there is
nothing to blush about: others would not
judge so. And I have no particular desire
to be set down as a young lady who is given
to throwing herself at the heads of men
who are not troubling themselves about
her. What would Germain think if he
heard it? Then what would my aunt say
if I came and asked her to let me marry
Germain—she who raves about title and dis-
tinction of birth and rank, who thinks very
little of other merits, or rather cannot be

induced to believe that real merits exists at
all apart from these advantages, who thinks
nothing is to be compared with them. Germain—who? she would ask. Why, the Germain who saved us, my mother and me,
when you left us to die. What a nice way
to curry favor that would be! She would
think that I was disposing very cleverly of
her fortune, and perhaps it would end by
my throwing her favors back to her. How
little it would cost me if in doing so I could
still retain her affection and cause her no
pain! Is there another in Paris or in
France who cares less for the world, or
riches, or style, than I do? Better a thousand times live good and happy in some retired little home than beat out your heart
and your life against the cold, tyrannical
breast of society. But my aunt's love I
must not lose if I can help it, and, besides,
I would feel some scruple in bringing Germain my heart only. If he knew and loved
me, he might think it enough; but, then, I
would not have the intense happines of en-
riching him. M. de Tourmagne says that it
is a hundred times easier for a rich man to

become learned than a poor one. The rich
man has more leisure, more repose of mind;
he has more opportunities of seeing varieties
of books, and countries, and people. Fancy
what a delight it would be to me to give my
philosopher all these advantages, what a
glory to raise the noble heart and mind of
him I love to a pedestal where all the world
might see and admire him, whence he might
speak to be gladly heard. No devoted heart
could be insensible to such hopes as these.
Science is my rival, my favored rival, and
yet so much do I love Germain, that I wish
with my own hands to deck my rival, and
adorn her and bring her to him. Since the
haughty dame must have money, and re-
serves her tenderest caresses for those of her
adorers who come to her with gold and dwell
in palaces, then the gold and the palace she
must have.

My first idea is to bring Germain to my
aunt's house without either him or her
knowing how it has been brought about; I
do not know yet how it will be brought
about; I see many obstacles, and yet I will
try. I want Madame d'Aubecourt to know

him and like him. Once she has seen him
(of course, without any suspicion of my
wishes), she will be sure to admire and like
him; I am proud of them both; I wish next
that, by my endeavors, Germain should make
a name for himself. M. de Tourmagne will
help me willingly and powerfully here. And
then I want Germain to see me sometimes
and speak to me, so that if he thinks of it at
all, he may think, "She is not plain, or stu-
pid, or silly." And when all this is done
we shall see further. Meanwhile I shall
speak to him and listen to him, and we shall
once more be friends. . . . Ah! I know
Elise will soon be sending me a little bitter
medicine in the shape of sensible advice. I
am afraid that sensible advice troubles me
without curing me.

IX.

MAY 29th.

My dearest Elise, since last I wrote to you
I had reason to think that my castles in the
air had received a shock which would overthrow them, never to ascend in their dreamy

beauty to the bright sky again. One day I saw a great fuss going on outside Germain's usually quiet house. People going to and fro and bringing all sorts of things including a great many ladies' nick-nacs, a work-table, a toilet-table, a flower-stand, etc. What if Germain was going to be married? Yesterday morning he came out with a bright elegant-looking girl leaning on his arm, to whom he was showing the most loving attention. He seemed quite a different person from the grave, quiet gentleman 1 was accustomed to meet. He laughed, chatted, and once he caught the hand lying on his arm, and then they laughed again. Of course, she must be his wife, and how happy they looked! Ah! my Lord Viscount de Sauveterre, never did you seem less pleasing to the object of your honored attentions than in the strong light of this simple, lost happiness. I put on my hat and went off to Mass. I knew that a quiet hour of prayer would do me all the good in the world. Germain and his companion were there before me, kneeling side by side. I knelt down very quietly behind them and

prayed for them with all my heart. But
by-and-by came a servant, who stopped
beside the young lady and spoke one of the
sweetest words I have ever heard in all my
life—"Mademoiselle!"—I wish I could pay
back that most excellent girl for the pleasure
she gave me at that moment. Mademoiselle
turned round and showed an unmistakable
family likeness to Germain. She was not
his wife, but simply his sister, who had come
to live with him, the sister who long ago
learned to love little Rœschen. She said a
word or two to her brother and then followed the servant. She had one of the
fairest young faces I have ever seen. A
bright, clever, good, wholesome face of some
twenty summers, that looked as if a frown
of bad temper had never crossed it, as if no
shade of evil could rest long upon it, a face,
in fact, quite in keeping with early Mass on
a glorious morning in May. In a short time
she came back with an old lady leaning on
her arm, for whom Germain busily prepared
a comfortable *prie-dieu*, and who, of course,
must be their mother. It was a rare sight,
Elise, when the moment of Communion

came, to see the three go up so reverently, the mother leaning on her noble son. I could not help feeling that I belonged to them; it seemed strange for me to be away alone, separated from them, and something seemed to tell me that God had wise ends in bringing us together again. I think we know our own in this world, Elise, and we stretch out our longing arms to them, and woe, woe, to us if we let wealth, or rank, or any other thing but duty thrust us apart; for I believe that just so shall we know them one day in heaven. My three friends made a very long thanksgiving, but not as long as mine; and I defy all their piety to make a more fervent one.

When I am in the church, these thoughts, far from distracting me, seem to gather up my whole will, my whole soul, into one earnest, refreshing prayer. It seems as if the shadow of the holy place fell across my heart, and that by the light of the sanctuary lamp my thoughts stole in; grave, calm, holy. Here God is my confidant, my counsellor, my guardian; and feelings that I would watch anxiously abroad in the world's glare, may here throw themselves down at his feet in all their strength, for with them goes the cry that they are all to be subject to the affair of salvation, and only important as they affect salvation. Do not be uneasy about me on this score. I have yesterday learned one consoling experience of my own spirit. I have seen that the final overthrow of all my hopes might crush my heart, but they could not root out resignation.

***

X.

JUNE 15th.

His name is Darcet—Darcet without a shade of an apostrophe. What a calamity! But really, now, it is not such an unbearable name after all. Perhaps my aunt will end by saying that it is just as good as Corbin: although Corbin, she thinks, is not without a certain heraldic rudeness, and breathes more of the antique than of the common-place. In a tournament given by the Duke of Brittany one Corbin of Anjou, master of the horse, exhibited much prowess—not a doubt but he was one of our Corbins. My dear Elise, can no one find a Darcet who fought in the Crusades, and buy my life's happiness with the dust of the ennobling dead? But, really, it is a shame for me to be satirical about my aunt, for I owe it to her that I have found out Germain's name.

Last evening the Curé came to spend the evening with us. I had remarked him on the previous day speaking to our friend in the street, and I bravely turned the conversation on the parishioners, asking him if he was content with their attendance. I knew well enough that this was a favorite topic with him, I knew how dearly he loved those who assi·ted regularly at all the devotions, and I knew that Germain and his mother and sister were models in this respect. Every Sunday they are in the church early, and in the evening they are in their places again before the bell has nearly done ringing for Vespers. I expected that the Curé would immediately cite such a splendid example, especially as poor M. de Tourmagne was there; and in spite of his real, sincere piety, the good count is wont to avoid High Mass in the most adroit manner, and very seldom makes his appearance at Vespers, or, when he does, it is generally towards the end of the *Magnificat.* Unfortunately, M. de Tourmagne guessed what was coming, and immediately flew to cover, and commenced an animated discussion on the subject of certain decrees and ordinances which prescribed assistance at all parish offices. So in punishment for my wickedness I was condemned to endure a shower of eloquence and erudition which I did not exactly bargain for. However, the gentlemen forgot themselves so far as to take to speaking Latin; my aunt lost all patience and plunged hotly into the argument on the side of the parish, reproaching M. de Tourmagne with having several times neglected to fast, because he was not in the church before the sermon to hear it announced. The count gave a parting stroke; he urged the active part men are at present obliged to play in civil society, the multiplication of occupation in consequence of the revolutions which have shaken Europe, and a hundred other arguments to the effect that the length of religious services are not in accordance with the present wants of civilization. Here I broke in, another opponent to the poor count's very fallacious arguments. I hinted that probably the Curé could cite some instances of persons whose occupations were as absorbing as those of M. de Tourmagne and who yet found time to come and join in the praises of God. "Certainly," ejaculated M. le Curé, "certainly;"—but that was all; we could see quite well that he was racking his brains to find an example; the fact was, none occurred to him, though this was exactly what I had counted on. My aunt, dreading that M. de Tourmagne should have the last word, came again to the rescue by assisting the pastor's ungrateful memory.

"For example," she said, "take that splendid young fellow who is there so regularly with his mother and sister;—you must have remarked them—near us, nearly under the pulpit. Stephanie, you know whom I mean?"

"Yes, aunt."

I became very intent, indeed, on my embroidery, for I felt the tell-tale color mounting uncomfortably into my face.

"You mean M. Darcet," cried the Curé, in delight, "M. Germain Darcet! Ah! my dear count, M. Darcet will condemn you. I forgot about him for the moment. A *savant* like yourself, but with his fortune and name to make and a mother and sister to support. That is occupation enough, I think, and still he never misses any of the devotions."

"*Darcet!*" repeated my aunt; "I do not know that family."

"It is not a family," replied the Curé, "at least not an aristocratic family; and yet they are three of the most charming people I have ever met. They are honor itself, and as to their piety, I have seldom met any so tender and solid."

"Germain Darcet!" repeated M. de Tourmagne, "Germain Darcet!—I wonder where I have heard that name before?"

"In the Academy of Science, most probably. M. Darcet is a most accomplished man. I believe he has written a book, but I don't think it has been successful;—he is too modest, and too proud to gain public admirers."

"Bah!" returned the count; "if he has

merit, believe me, the admirers will come of themselves. Darcet!—Darcet!—I am sure I have heard that name before. What is his occupation?"

"I don't know. He speaks very little about himself. I only know that he has travelled a good deal. But that reminds me, Madame d'Aubecourt—he is a country-man of yours;—he is a Vendéan."

"Oh, well," said my aunt, "I do not wonder at his piety then. Good blood never lies, true blue never stains."

"Yes," added the Curé; "his father was a gentleman of some property, whose dearest object in life was to bring up his noble son worthily, and whose only regret was that he had not more money to leave him With the consent of his excellent mother, our young friend set off on his travels, and by his hard work he supplies for the deficiencies of their slender income."

Here the conversation changed, very much against my will, you may be sure. But this was not to be the last time that the name of Germain Darcet was to be introduced in conversation in the *salon* of the Marchioness

d'Aubecourt. And he is a Vendéan! Elise,
Elise, the ways of Providence are very
wonderful. Good-bye, now, for I am off to
our bookseller's, stricken with a new and
most brilliant idea which ought to have
occurred to my mind long ago.

XL

JUNE 16th.

I am now going to tell you what happened
at the bookseller's, and I claim your kindly
admiration for the ingenuity I there dis-
played. Having selected some of the best
new books for my aunt, I inquired if they
had any book by M. Germain Darcet.

"What title, mademoiselle?" asked the
man.

"I do not know the title," I answered.

He murmured "Germain Darcet" once
or twice, as if trying to awaken his memory;
and I was thinking sadly that the poor
fellow must be very little known. Then he
produced a catalogue, and after turning over
the leaves, he suddenly seized a ladder,
planted it against a distant bookcase, and

from a very high shelf too, a very large
book, from which he blew the dust vigor-
ously. "The Pharaohs: Fragments of a
Journey in Egypt. By Germain Darcet,"
he read, "this is it, I suppose, mademoiselle." I asked if he had written any other
work, and being answered in the negative, I
caught up my treasure, gave the sum de-
manded, and went my way. "The very
thing to awaken M. de Tourmagne's interest,"
I thought, as I flew along at my usual pace
when I am full of some new scheme; keeping time with my thoughts—"anything
about old hieroglyphics for him." A glance
showed me that the pages were thickly
strewn with Latin, Greek, and German,
besides quotations in some queer-looking
characters, which I supposed to be either
Hebrew or Egyptian; and nevertheless, I
determined that I would not sleep that night
until I had read every word of it. I assure
you, I did really read every word of it with
the greatest pleasure, the Hebrew and Greek
always excepted; the Latin was not quite a
sealed book to me, and I did my best to make
out what the authors said whom Germain

had honored by quoting. But my efforts in mastering such a heap of science were not quite so praiseworthy as they might at first appear; for although the book was scientific in the extreme, although it soared high above my poor capacity, I still caught glimpses of the author himself which lit up the dark page and made my study a labor of love. Many of the little details of his travels were told in Germain's own voice; and in the introduction its tones rose very high in defending religion against the errors and heresies of M. Volney, whom I know nothing about, but whom he spoke of as an enemy of Christianity. You would be delighted with it. Then he describes the dangers he has gone through in those frightful countries, and describes the misery of the inhabitants in most touching terms. The whole is full of little traits and anecdotes which I knew would please my aunt; and as for M. Tourmagne, the book would be a very garden of delights for him. Then, liking the book, he would like the writer. I like him, I know, though I do not belong to the Academy of Science.

XII.

JUNE 18th.

There is nothing particular going on to-day, M. de Tourmagne is gone to the country for a week or so, and has not yet received my present of the " Pharaohs; " but to-morrow, I think, something important will happen, for—. But wait, Elise, until I have told you the whole affair, and I think you will agree with me that it looks as if God were pointing out my destiny.

We wanted a housekeeper, and I asked M. le Curé if he could recommend anyone to us. He said that he thought he could, and this morning came a person of about forty years of age, rather sad-looking, but I am sure very good, who turned out to suit me better than I had expected. She was a widow, she said, and had once occupied a much better position than her present one, but was now obliged to go to service in order to support her children. I thought of my mother, and had all but said that we would employ her, when it occurred to me that it might be advisable to have further reference, and I asked her to name some friend of whom we could inquire about her. "I have known a Madame Darcet, who lives near here for a very long time; I am a countrywoman of hers, and she is charitably taking care of my little child whilst I look for a situation."

I said that I was certain my aunt would think Madame Darcet's recommendation conclusive, and that I would speak to her on the subject. I then dismissed the aspirant and went to paint her picture in very glowing colors for Madame d'Aubecourt.

"Of course you will take her at once," she said, when she had heard all.

"I think so," I answered, "but M. le Curé is rather easily taken in, especially by a tale of woe, and perhaps it would be well to have some further particulars. Madame Darcet knows her, and is taking care of one of her children, so we could send to her for information."

"What a charming, charitable woman this Madame Darcet must be;—taking care of her child. Why that speaks very well for her son who provides for it. He must be a very fine character."

I allowed my aunt to continue her vein of praise, unchecked, and when she had quite done I asked her whom she would send to Madame Darcet.

"Whom? why, yourself, of course, Stephanie." I made no objection; but, after this little dialogue, I had some trouble in keeping myself from getting absent. My aunt, however, did not remark it. She commenced giving me a little lecture in domestic economy, warning me of the great responsibility which devolves on the mistress of a household and the necessity of inquiring into the character of domestics, especially those employed in so onerous a situation as that of housekeeper, who has so many valuables and plate and linen under her care. The old Marchioness d'Aubecourt, her mother-in-law, was wont, she said, to make it her duty to inspect her establishment from cellar to garret every day—a practice which she would gladly emulate, did her health permit her to do so. The digression ended with an assurance that the recommendation of so virtuous and excellent a lady as Madame Darcet would be entirely satisfactory and convincing. At

which point I took my eyes off a lilac-tree in
the garden, at which I had been gazing
rather dreamily, and tried to look as if I had
been all the time deeply attentive to what
she had said. After a few further remarks
I withdrew, having a vague idea that Madame
the Marchioness, who is at times somewhat
subject to *ennui*, was not sorry to have an
opportunity of hearing some details of our
amiable neighbors. However, in discerning
the beam in her eye, I must not overlook the
mote in my own, for I am quite as anxious
as my aunt is to know more of the quiet, old
house opposite, and I can hardly believe that
to-morrow I shall make Mme. Darcet's acquaintance. I wish to-morrow was come;
but what if I should meet Germain? I
tremble when I think of that, and almost
wish I was not going;—and yet I am longing
to go. When we have been longing very, very
much for something, especially a beloved
presence, and when we have watched, and
waited, and counted the days until our happiness, it often happens that as the thing
comes into our very grasp, a strong, wild
desire comes over us to turn and fly away. I
feel just so about to-morrow's visit.

It is a long time since I said anything about the Viscount de Sauveterre. We see him quite often enough, I assure you, but he does not rise in the least in my favor, and if I am not very much mistaken he is falling a little in that of my aunt. I do my best to assist his fall, a little treacherously sometimes, I fear. This is how I proceed:—The viscount is very fond of showing off his wit, of which, as far as a flashy sort of wit goes, he has some, but in his haste he does not always pause to weigh his words. He chatters away, and I listen with my eyes on my work, knowing that there is no immediate necessity for interrupting him. I have measured his character exactly and weighed it against my aunt's particular antipathies, and by means of a little word dropped cleverly here and there I manage to keep him on subjects which I know will jar most upon her taste. As long as he runs on in this way, I encourage him with a smile and an air of deepest attention; but the moment he gets on the road to favor, I hasten to draw him back again. His prime error being that I am the only one he has to charm,

I lead him as I choose. Poor fellow, he is
not solitary in supposing that the beloved
one is the only power to be conciliated, overlooking the strong hands that in reality hold
the reins of fate. I could forgive the viscount his somewhat interested endeavors to
please and dazzle me, if I was not afraid of
the more formidable abilities of his mother,
on whom I have no mercy. One look at her
cold, haughty face, and any shadow of
scruple disappears from my mind. Deceit
is my only weapon of defence; one must be
snaky to baffle a snake. And so I go on,
drawing the unfortunate viscount into the
most absurd blunders, whilst he imagines
he is getting on splendidly. Occasionally he
plays the liberal, believing that I nourish a
secret admiration for the opinions of M. Ben-
jamin Constant. And into these conversa-
tions he throws himself heart and soul.
Madame de Sauveterre I lead by a different
way. She must be got to talk, and fume,
and chatter, about the noble blood of the
Caniacs of Perigord; and I manage con-
stantly, but without appearing to do so, to
bring her round to the subject of common

people, low marriages, etc. My aunt, though
at starting somewhat of her opinions, soon
begins to chafe; and I begin to hope—I
hardly know what.

XIII.

JUNE 19th.

It was with a beating heart that I set out
this morning to pay my visit to Madame
Darcet. I dreaded meeting Germain, and I
trembled at the mere possibility of his
opening the door for me. In the streets and
roads I could meet him with the greatest
pleasure; for ten to one, he would be absorbed in a book or looking straight before
him, and it would not matter whether I was
blushing up to the roots of my hair or not.
But when I should be face to face with him,
and have to speak, it would be a very different affair. However, the thing had to be
done, and I walked bravely through the
garden gate, and found myself in just such
a little court as you see in a huudred nice
old places in Paris. There was a beautiful
old well, shaded by a Bohemian olive, with an

old-fashioned railing of wrought-iron work running round it, covered with clinging hops and honeysuckles. Clusters of wall-flowers bloomed on the walls, and a vine, flinging its soft green arms over half the building. Away at the end of the court, through a little gate which opens under two immense lilacs, shone a vista of mignonette, and jasmine, and clematis, and roses, spreading away in breadths of fragrance under the bright sun. Birds were singing gaily in a cage suspended before the old *loge du concierge*, and a big cat, dozing on the parapet of the well, divided a fragment of sleepy attention between them and some hens which were picking at the grass springing between the flags of the court not far off. It was the very ideal of a sage's retreat. I must say I have a friendly feeling for men who choose these silent, flowery mansions for the scene of their home-life.

I crossed the court and went up a pretty staircase lighted by windows which showed glimpses of bloom through curtains of that graceful, obtrusive vine. Arrived at the first floor, I rang, and waited with awful com-

posure for the answer. A slow step was
heard approaching, the door opened, and
Madame Darcet herself stood before me,
leaning on the shoulder of a little girl, who
pressed up to her and looked at me with
wide blue eyes. The graceful little thing
held an open book in her hand, and Madame
Darcet had not waited to remove her specta-
cles; all of which showed me that I had
interrupted a reading lesson. I was strongly
reminded of an Italian picture I had seen of
St. Anne and the little Virgin. Madame
Darcet looked somewhat surprised when she
saw me, and became more so when I hurriedly told my aunt's name and requested a
few minutes' conversation. She took me into
a large, sombre room, apologizing that she
could not bring me into the drawing-room
as there were workmen there. A glance
around told me that I was in Germain's
study. There was a large bureau in one
corner covered with papers, and globes, and
Eastern curiosities, and heaps of books; but
there was no student, which, I assure you,
was a great relief. That fact, and the
charming manner of the dear old lady put

me quite at my ease, and I told my errand
bravely, glancing about the room as I did
so. Madame Darcet gave a very high character to her *protégée*, saying that the only
fault she knew her to have was that she was
a little too fond of talking. I did not feel
very much distressed at hearing of this predilection.

I chatted away, asking question after
question, at the imminent danger of saying
something rash, for I was in hopes that
Mademoiselle Darcet would make her appearance, and I did not wish to go away
until I had seen her. All my questions
were answered gently and patiently. I was
over and over again assured that our new
housekeeper was quite a treasure. I did not
entertain the slightest doubt about her, only
Mademoiselle Darcet had not come. I asked
Madame Darcet if the little girl whom I had
seen with her was the daughter of the person
in question. "Yes," she told me, "we took
her one time, when she was delicate, and we
have kept her ever since."

"I think," said I, "that my aunt would
like to take her to be with her mother."

"We would not wish," she said, "to deprive the poor child of such an opportunity, but we shall be very sorry to lose her; my daughter is very fond of her, and her pretty ways amuse my son very much."

"Your son's pursuits appear to be of a very serious nature," I said, with a glance towards the globes and the awful-looking books.

"Yes, very serious, and very thankless too, dear," she said, with a sad little smile; "but his hopes and his spirit are centred in them. If I have not the joy of seeing him famous, I have at least the happiness of seeing him content."

I felt in that moment how gladly I would give my wealth to buy him the position he deserved; I felt an almost irresistible inclination to tell that loving mother that I was eager to do my part to make him all that he had a right to be, and how much the rich niece of Madame d'Aubecourt could do. At last I rose, and said politely: "The world, madame, often passes by the greatest merit, but God never overlooks virtue."

"That is true, dear," said Madame Darcet, rising also; and we went out together.

What little chances seem to turn the scale of our destinies at the most important moment: or rather, not chances, but little touches from the hand of Providence leading us on in the way we are to go. When the outer door was opened, we were greeted by a loud clap of thunder. A cloud which had been spreading and darkening over the sky had burst now into a sudden summer storm, and great floods of rain came sweeping down on the drenched court. Madame Darcet, of course, could not let me venture out, so we went back to the study and continued our chat. I asked her how she liked our parish; she said, smilingly, that she never disliked any place but Smyrna. I gave an exclamation of surprise. She then told me that she had had the courage to set out alone for Smyrna when her son was very ill there; and, drawn into the dear subject, she went on and on of herself to tell me a thousand things about Germain, to which I listened with the greatest delight. She told me that she had left her own country, and a sister who was a great comfort to her, to come to Paris, because Germain was leading such

an isolated life alone. I praised her affection, but added that all this changing, etc.,
must be very hard on one of her time of
life. "Oh, but such a son as mine makes
up for everything," she said, with a sort of
sweet pride. "When I think of the long
years he passed in all sorts of danger, and
through which I suffered the most harrow-
ing anxiety, the exquisite joy of our first re-
union comes back to me with all its sweetness, and I forget everything but the happiness of having him safe beside me." I remarked that it was astonishing that she
should ever let him leave her. "You are
right," she said, "and believe me, I did my
best to dissuade him, but I came in the end
to think it was God's will that he should go.
He is like one of those wild plants that only
strengthen and flourish in the storm. He
would rust and grow restless in the monot-
ony of ordinary life. And, besides, I believe
now that he acted rightly in going. The
knowledge which he has heaped together
with so much trouble will serve to increase
the glory of religion, and, perhaps, by-
and-by, his own." All this was most de-

lightful to me, and I did not care to let the
conversation flag. I expressed a hope that
she was now freed from all her anxieties.
"My son and daughter," she went on,
"form a little paradise for me, and we are
just as happily united, and just as tranquilly
at home here as we ever were in our own
most peaceful province. My daughter studies
and helps me with the housekeeping; Germain works; the little one learns to read, and
in the evening we all enjoy ourselves, and are
very happy. People never seem to dream or
understand how happy it is possible to be at
a very little cost."

"I am not one of those people," I said,
suddenly and sharply, for the picture she
had just drawn roused up anew that longing
which seemed almost a demand of right to be
one of them, to be something to them, to do
something for them. She looked at me
with a little astonishment, but very kindly,
that mother whose child I would proudly
be, and I turned my head away, partly to
drive back an indiscreet mist which had
gathered before my eyes, and partly to hide
my real feelings, and began another scrutiny

of that most interesting room. It certainly
was stamped with its owner's character.
Over his bureau hung a crucifix, and near it
were the arms which he had borne in his
strange travels, when he had been obliged to
adopt the Asiatic costume. In another place
hung the portraits of his mother and sister,
with last Palm Sunday's holy branch between
them. These, with the heaped-up books
below, seemed to tell what Germain was: so
good, so learned, so loving; such a man, such
a son, such a brother! But two other objects attracted my attention, which were the
means of my learning more of Madame
Darcet's son, and of drawing me on to a
step which is likely to wield a very decisive
influence over my fate. One was a group of
flowers, exquisitely painted; the other was a
sampler, such as little girls learn to mark
on, bearing the twenty-four letters, the ten
figures, and, to finish out the canvas, on one
side a bird, and on the other an object intended to represent a shrub; it was framed
with little gilt rods, rather the worse of the
wear. The sight of this latter piece of rub-
bish in a philosopher's study made me smile

as I turned towards Madame Darcet, and
said : "This is some of your daughter's first
handiwork, I presume;—and are the pretty
flowers from her hand also ?"

" No," she answered; " they are not hers,
but I think they are almost as dear to Germain as if they were. There are *souvenirs*
of one of the happiest times in his life.
Those flowers were painted for him by a
German lady who is dead now, but whom
he had the happiness of assisting in the
most dreadful reverses of fortune."

"And the marker ?" I whispered.

" The marker was worked for him by the
lady's little daughter, a dear child, to whom
he was like a sort of adopted father. We
never could find out what became of the
poor little thing. Germain grieved after
her as if she had been his own sister. Sometimes," she added, smilingly, "when I speak
to him of my wish to see him happily married, he laughs, and says: 'Who knows, if
little Rœschen had not disappeared we might
have fulfilled a certain little engagement we
once made, but I have seen no one else I
could care for.' It appears that the child,

to show her love for him, used to say that
when she was big enough she would be his
wife." She turned towards me, but the
smile died away on her lips as she caught
sight of my face. "My dear child," she
cried, starting up, "are you ill? You look
as if you were going to faint." The storm
was over, and she hastened to open the
window, letting a dewy, fragrant breath
float in from the refreshed garden, across
her dear figure and her sweet, kind face.
Then she wanted to call my maid, who was
waiting in another room; but I passed my
hand across my forehead, and said quickly:
"Oh, no, I am better now, thank you, and I
never faint. Come and sit by me." She
came, taking both my hands softly in hers,
and then I said: "I am going to tell you a
great secret, but I ask you by all that you
hold dear, by your love for Germain, to keep
it as long as I ask you."

"Yes, dear," she promised, in surprise, "I
will keep any secret you think fit to confide
in me."

"Well," I said;—"but first tell me, was
the little girl of whom we have just spoken
called Rosalie Corbin?"

"Yes," she answered, in amazement, "that was her name."

"And I am Rosalie," I cried, stretching out my arms to her, "Rosalie, come back living and full of gratitude, and only longing to call you mother."

"My child," she cried, clasping m in her arms, "my dear child, how glad Germain will be."

The fragrant air came floating into the quiet room—Germain's room. All was so peaceful and sweet, with the silence only broken by the distant twittering of the birds, and the soothing voice of Germain's mother, calling me her child, her dear child. I felt so tired, and here was such perfect rest. Must I go away, and, perhaps, marry the Viscount de Sauveterre, and never speak to them, never be happy again? I slid down from my seat, and in another moment was on my knees before her, my arms round her waist, and my head on her breast, telling her all. How I had been harassed by the thought of marrying against my will, such a man as M. de Sauveterre, merely for position; how Germain had been my hero, my beau-ideal;

how in trying to find him I had come on his letter to my mother; in a word, everything that I have told, you. She kissed me over and over again, and said that she had often wished to see her son married, and that she would be glad to win "little Rœschen" for his wife. "Germain must know nothing, of course," I went on, "to him as well as to everyone but you, I must still be merely Madame d'Aubecourt's niece. My plan is to make him happy, not to disturb him. If he comes to care for me, and I succeed in getting my aunt to agree, which will be difficult, but not impossible, then all will be well. If all fails, he will be simply no better nor no worse than before. As to me, I love him, and I shall never marry anyone else. The worst that can happen me is to stay with my aunt as I am, and we are very happy together, and perhaps afterwards I would end my days in a convent: a future which, I assure you, seems anything but distasteful to me. God will always help me to bear any disappointments; for in all this His glory and my own salvation have always been my first thought." She smiled affectionately at my sketch of a probable future, and then she stroked my cheek and said that she thought God was very good in sending her such a dear child, and that she hoped there was great happiness in store for her son; and I promised to consult her to the utmost of my power as I went along. "And now," I said, "I should like so much to see your daughter; is she not at home?"

"Jeanne is with your new housekeeper, who has told her of two or three sick people, neighbors of hers, who were in great want, and she is gone to see what she can do for them. She will be away some time, and I expect Germain in every moment."

"Then let me go," I cried, starting up, with my face in a blaze. "If I were to see him now I should feel as if I had done something bold, and——"

"No, dear," she interrupted, with her arm round my shoulders, "there is nothing but good in what you have done; there is a Providence in everything."

"Then could you come with me to the house where your daughter is?" I asked. "I might tell your *protégée* that we have

decided to engage her, and then we can all
come back together."

She agreed, and we went, I feeling very
proud to have her lean on my strong, young
arm as we went down the staircase. Meanwhile my maid called a hackney coach, and
we were soon at our destination. I could
have imagined myself coming into the
wretched garret where my father died, for
it was just such another miserable place.
The housekeeper was supporting the poor,
sick woman near the window, that she might
get a little fresh air and sunshine, and
Mademoiselle Darcet was making the bed.
I have often visited the sick, and always
with great pleasure, but I had never strung
my charity up to such a pitch as this; and
the graceful air of contentment with which
the young girl went about her task very
much increased the admiration I already
had for her. When I had told my errand,
which seemed to delight her assistant very
much, I helped in the making of the bed,
and then we put the poor woman back again
and made her quite comfortable, at which
she thanked us extremely and promised to
pray for us. I emptied my purse into

Jeanne's hands, who thought me remark-
ably generous, and then I took the two
ladies home. I hope that Jeanne and I
have only commenced a very fast friendship.
She is delightful. You could not imagine
anyone more simple or more charming.
She has such a vivid way of saying things,
whether grave or gay, that they go straight
to your heart. Certainly, God has blessed
Madame Darcet in her children.

So now, dear Elise, I have come to the
end of a long story and a serious adventure,
and, rash or impulsive as I may have been,
I cannot regret it. As Madame Darcet says,
there is a Providence in all things, and there
was a Providence in my burst of confidence
to-day. But there is still more to tell. This
evening closed with a conversation almost
equally important. To-morrow I shall write
you an account of it.

XIV.

JUNE 20th.

Yesterday after dinner I gave Madame
d'Aubecourt an interesting account of my
visits to Madame Darcet first, and then to

the housekeeper. She was charmed with all I told her of them all—of Madame Darcet's goodness, Germain's grand character, and Jeanne's charity. She gave me as much money as I could wish for the poor invalid; and she added, what was equally pleasing to me, that, as I seemed to have taken particular fancy to Jeanne, she would be very glad to see me make a friend of her. This last speech of my aunt's need not surprise you; for, though she is very proud, she is also confiding, enthusiastic, and good; besides, she is always afraid of my being lonely, and she is very fond of good people when she meets them. She would be glad to see me make an intimate friend of my charming Jeanne as long as she remained in ignorance of my plans with regard to the *roturier* Germain. We were chatting away most delightfully and enjoying ourselves very much indeed, when Madame de Sauveterre and the viscount were announced. You must allow, my dear Elise, that it was at least provoking; and I think I may confess to very uncharitable feelings towards them for choosing that moment for their visit. What did they

want? I thought; what were they going to
do? Why must they always come like black
shadows falling across the brightness of my
life? And I felt that the noble lady and
her son had done me great injury, and I fear
that I made up my mind to watch for an
occasion to be avenged. I had not long to
wait. Some other people arrived, and the
conversation turned on a young marchioness
who had lately been presented at court, where
she showed some pride of her *couronne à
trefles*, and who was merely a Mademoiselle
Corbec, daughter of a Norman notary. The
blood of the Caniacs rose. I, seeing my
advantage, gave a little touch of the spur;
and the storm of sarcasm burst over our
devoted heads. Between Corbec the notary
and Corbin the attorney there is not a very
vast difference, and Madame de Sauveterre's
hailstones, powerless to hurt the absent Corbec, fell painfully about the head of Madame
the Marchioness d'Aubecourt, and wounded
her sadly. I saw how she felt it, and I was
very sorry for her; but Madame de Sauveterre was only warming to her subject. A
look from her son, who turned pale as he at

last fathomed Madame d'Aubecourt's evident
annoyance, warned her too late. With Corbec still on her lips, Corbin rushed into her
memory. What a figure she cut when her
eyes fell on my aunt's marble face. She lost
her presence of mind completely, reddened,
stammered, heaped blunder on blunder, and
finally retired with her son, without having
at all recovered her equilibrium. My exas-
perated aunt could hardly contain herself
until they were in the anteroom. "What a
fop! and what a fool!" she ejaculated; I
said nothing. "You might forgive such
outlandish pride," she went on, "if they left
their victims to the shelter of their harmless,
if obscure, origin. But no; there is nothing
that their boasted heraldry would not stoop
to, that they might gain the gold of the very
plebeians they despise."

"Yes," I answered, "I do not think the
Caniacs of Perigord would feel called upon
to rise from the tomb in indignation if M.
Corbec had dared to offer his daughter and
her million to the Viscount de Sauveterre."

"No, indeed," she cried; "and they would
soon have been found dancing attendance in
the notary's office."

"Madame de Sauveterre's vanity is really amusing," I went on; "and yet I cannot help pitying her when I see how she deprives herself of the love and esteem of so many good and lovable people, simply because their origin is not sufficiently noble. If my uncle, Monsieur the Marquis d'Aubecourt, had held such opinions as hers, he should never have known my grandfather, and so, have probably lost his life, or at least his happiness." It was with fear and trembling, and with my arms round her neck, that I ventured on this last consideration; but my aunt took it very well. "You are a true Corbin," she said, "and you know that nobility like my husband's is worth that of all the Caniacs in the world. There is a nobility of blood and name, of course, but there is also a nobility of the soul, which is goodness. Do you not think that such a woman as Madame Darcet, for instance, is a thousand times more truly noble than the ambitious Countess de Sauveterre—and d'Escarbagnas?"

"Madame Darcet, certainly, has the advantage in this way."

"And her son," she went on, "how much superior to that little fool of a Viscount, who pretends to ape the advanced radical."

I assure you these last words overwhelmed me with joy. I was on the point of unbosoming myself at full length about M. Darcet; but, satisfied with seeing Madame de Sauveterre and her precious son out of the race, I wisely held my tongue. My aunt is not yet completely cured of her aristocratic proclivities. I know her well. Great things must come to pass before Corbin wins the day from d'Aubecourt.

XV.

JUNE 22d.

M. de Tourmagne has come back at last. As soon as he had paid his respects to Madame d'Aubecourt, I carried him off into a corner to have a talk with him, and to lecture him about looking so tired and done up after his trip. I told him it was both wrong and foolish of him to take his ambition with him to the country, and, instead of getting up his health, to spend himself on hard work and come back quite pale. He likes me to show an interest in him in this way, although he is perfectly assured of my constant affection for him; and he now acknowledged that he had been racking his brains and breaking his heart over some unfortunate, half-effaced inscription which some one had wrongly interpreted and murdered.

"If it had been an Egyptian inscription," I said, thoughtfully, "I might have helped you."

"You?" he cried, laughing outright.

"Yes," I answered in the same tone. "Tell me, M. le Comte, does your inscription relate to a Ptolemy or a Zodiac? Does it come from Memphis or from Thebes? For behold, I have had a whole regiment of Pharaohs in my room for eight days, whom I shall question with much pleasure on any subject you wish."

"Well, it is precisely to the zodiac that it refers," he answered.

"The little zodiac, no doubt?" I went on, "it is so perplexing."

"And the great zodiac does not puzzle you at all, I presume?" he laughed.

"Not at all," I returned. "Do not fancy for a moment that I believe all M. Depuis' cock-and-bull stories. Why, he is ignorant of the very rudiments of phonetic writing. All that he says of the great zodiac is deserving of no more credence than the genealogy of a Caniac of Limousin. As to the little zodiac: do you know that it is neither fifteen thousand years old, nor eight thousand years old, nor even eighteen hundred years old, but was invented by a Roman consul about a hundred years posterior to the Christian era?"

"Can you prove that?" he cried, with an eager gravity, which made me smile, though it delighted me.

"Certainly," I replied; "one Greek word settles the question."

"What word?"

"Ah! unfortunately I cannot read it, but you are more happy. I shall show it to you.

I ran up stairs and brought him Germain's book. "Now, Monsieur de Tourmagne," I said, entering the room; "you accuse me of never thinking of you when you are out of sight, and yet here is a book that I bought.

for you while you were away. It speaks of
the zodiac at page 500, and gives both M.
Depuis and M. de Volney their due."

My dear Elise, it is a terrible thing to have
a secret to keep. No sooner had he read the
title and the author's name than M. de Tourmagne bent on my face such a searching look,
or what appeared to me as such, that it dis-
concerted me extremely, and I have thought
over it, and wondered at it ever since. However, I recovered myself quickly. "I am not
going to fall out with you about the price,
Monsieur le Comte," I said, gaily; "all I ask
in return is the little china god which you
refused me some time ago, so that having
duly steeped it in holy water, I may place it
on my mantelpiece as a souvenir of you."

"It seems to be a very learned work," he
said, turning over the pages; "I wonder that
I have never heard of it, or seen it before.
However, it turns up in the nick of time for
me, and you shall have the china god, my
dear Stephanie."

"How glad I am," I cried; "not so much
for the god, as that you must always be my
friend now."

"Rest assured of that, Stephanie," he said, very gravely. "But tell me, dear child, did you read the whole of this book?"

"Yes," I answered, "and found it very interesting. Besides, I wanted to see if it were difficult enough and incomprehensible enough to be offered to you, and I was bent on having the china god."

"Even so," went on M. de Tourmagne, "the book is full of Greek and mathematics, and I must congratulate the author who knows how to make such subjects palatable."

I was getting audacious, and even this shaft failed to disconcert me.

"Listen, M. de Tourmagne," I said, confidentially, "I know Madame Darcet, and find her everything that is nice and good. I wish you would interest yourself in her clever son."

"Indeed, I shall be very glad to do so," said the count, heartily. "The book is curious and well written, and is in itself quite a letter of introduction."

I could have embraced him for being so good. I was almost afraid to say a word of thanks, lest I should say more than I wished just then. He is very shrewd, but I think I am nearly as much so. After all, however, perhaps it would not be such a dreadful affair if he did suspect something. He is not particularly enthralled by the attractions of either Caniac or De Sauveterre. He is kind, prudent, wise, and very fond of me. I shrink from it just now, and yet I cannot help feeling that I should be glad to trust M. de Tourmagne.

XVI.

JUNE 25th.

I overtook Jeanne and her mother this morning coming from Mass, and walked with them, talking of the poor, sick old woman, who has been removed to a good hospital for incurables, where, I think, she will end her days in peace. I asked Madame Darcet to allow me to take Jeanne away with me, to which both gladly consented; for Jeanne seems to have taken as great a fancy to me as I have to her. I managed to whisper to Madame Darcet that everything was going on well, and then Jeanne and I went off together in great spirits to the Hotel d'Aubecourt. As we passed the threshold I felt as if I had gained a great victory and made a breach through which Germain must soon follow.

Success put me in good spirits; my gaiety infected Jeanne, and we chattered away like two magpies. However, a true conspirator never loses sight of his design; and I soon brought my new friend round to the subject of her own family. She is a very prudent young lady, and a little reticent, but still I managed to bring out several little facts about her beloved brother which I intended to turn to good account. Germain supports the family, almost entirely by his own exertion. In order to make money he works incessantly for the printers at Latin and Greek books, which give him a great deal of fatigue, and prevent him from finishing a great work which he has been engaged on for some time, and which is the centre of many of his dreams of ambition.

"Germain has been rather unfortunate," went on Jeanne; "his first book was not successful; it was full of the names of great men whose opinions he opposed, and this made the libraries very cool about it. He might, of course, have gone here and there, and written to the papers and asked every-one's assistance, but he had neither the time nor the inclination to do so."

"That must have discouraged him very much?"

"Discouraged him!" she laughed, in her bright, merry way; "he discouraged!—no; I think that word is almost unknown in our family. He says that a *savant* does not de-serve to be recognized until he is at least gray, if not bald. We go our way, and say like the charcoal-burners when they are black, '*C'est le mêtier qui veut cela*' ('It is the nature of the trade'), and then we are so happy among ourselves; and we have all our own work to do in the household. Ger-main makes money; my mother manages it; I help her about the house, study, and make fun, which last, I assure you, is most useful to a *savant.* You must not think me boast-ing; but really, sadness and *ennui* are as little known in our house as discourage-ment."

"Who would have it in their power to be of use to your brother?" I asked next.

"The minister of public instruction, I believe, but I am not quite sure," was the answer. "I think he asked him to have the book printed at the royal *Imprimerie;* but he got no answer, which, perhaps, was natural, as they knew nothing about him, and he had to print it himself."

We spoke of other things, of a number of other things; for I was anxious that Jeanne should forget how much she had told me, and then we parted, mutually delighted with our chat. Now, dear Elise, my own true friend, you know all. The minister of public instruction is a relation of yours, and he can be of the greatest use to M. Germain Darcet, author of the valuable book called the "Pharaohs," who lives in Paris, Rue No——? Quick, quick, Elise, write at once; beg, pray, arrange, tease, until Germain draws some fruit from my gratitude and your goodness. I read the other day in a paper of some book which the minister had bought up for all the royal libraries. I do not remember what book it was, and I am sure I wish it all success—only it was not my "Pharaohs." And can nothing be done for these neglected sovereigns? Whatever else they deserved, it has generally been allowed to them that they have the right of honorable sepulture. Seriously, the minister has a thousand means in his power for helping a young author. He could give him a pension, he could present him to the king, he could get him a place, he could have him appointed to a post in the royal *Imprimerie*. Oh! if I were minister, I would soon draw down the blessings of Jeanne and Rœschen on my devoted head. But I leave all to your true heart. As to papers— Madame d'Aubecourt's steward has lately begged her patronage and mine for a relation of his who is a journalist. We shall see if he cannot be induced to write a nice article. Of course you are laughing at me, and certainly, I have as many plans in my head as a character in a comedy.

XVII

JULY 1st.

Many, many thanks for all your goodness, my own dear Elise, and it is all that I have to console me in a new uneasiness which God has sent me.

This morning my maid brought me a paper
which the steward had given her for me. I
opened it and found a long article of eulogy
on M. Darcet's book. It was such a learned
work, so well written, so interesting, so full
of novelty; in fact, I think that I myself
could have hardly found anything to add.
The journalist, who was so very favorable in
his judgments of the works of my friends,
may count on the patronage of my aunt. I
felt quite delighted with my success, the
more so as I could congratulate myself that
I had acted with the greatest discretion in
the matter, and I was just fancying to myself
the pleasure which Madame Darcet, and
perhaps even the stoical Germain himself,
would have in reading it, when my eyes fell
on another paragraph, and I read that the
king was about to raise to the dignity of a
peer of France—whom do you think?—M.
de Sauveterre. I could hardly believe my
eyes. I had read the article about Germain twice over; but I think I read this
at least ten times. Oh! these de Sauveterres, these de Sauveterres! am I never
to be rid of them? I am sure I wish them

no ill; but, really, the king has chosen a most unlucky moment for dispensing his favors. If Madame de Sauveterre, in her new rank, still continues to cherish the same intentions with regard to me, or rather my dowry, the king has put into her hands the power of gaining higher favor with my aunt than obliterating the impression of her impertinence of the other evening. How could my aunt ever endure to see me refuse to become a peeress? The peerage will descend to the Viscount Henri in his turn, and what a solidity the brilliant perspective will give to his character in Madame d'Aubecourt's eyes. He may play the *Jacobin* as he pleases now, and it will only arise from a charming thoughtlessness, which anyone can foresee time will correct. If there is a fault in acknowledging such opinions, he does not mean it, that is all.

However, dear Elise, it must be all as God sees best. One sure and consoling thought is, that the king may make as many peers of France as ever he likes, but he cannot force me to marry them. If Madame de Sauveterre comes to upset my projects, I shall not scruple to do my very best to destroy hers.

Now, I shall send that most mysterious of persons, our new housekeeper, to take the paper to Madame Darcet, and give her, I hope, a happy day. She will build all sorts of bright castles on the eulogy on the " Pharaohs," and she will read the two lines about M. de Sauveterre, the serpent under the flowers which threatens to destroy all our hopes.

XVIII.

JULY 3d.

I was beginning to grow uneasy at M. de Tourmagne's long silence on the subject of the " Pharaohs; " so this morning I took courage, and began: " Monsieur le Comte, did you not care for my book? You have never said a word about it."

" What book, dear? " he asked.

" The book about the zodiac."

" Oh! Monsieur Darcet's book you mean. I dine with the author this evening."

" I did not know that you were acquainted with M. Darcet," I said.

My dear Elise, it is really admirable how
I keep my countenance during such dia-
logues as these. When I experience any
little shock, I generally manage to recover
myself before I speak again. However, M.
de Tourmagne's next remarks this morning
put my equanimity to a very severe test.
"We have lately become acquainted," was
the answer; "his book spoke so very well
for him that I had some curiosity in knowing whether it told truth or not."

"Well?" I said, in perhaps rather an
anxious voice.

"Well," went on M. de Tourmagne,
wickedly, "a book is not always to be relied
upon as a picture of the writer's character.
They paint in very glowing and often in very
deceptive colors; so that frequently on seek-
ing to know the mind from which such
beauties emanate we find, instead of a hero
of depth of mind and generosity, a puffed
up scribbler of most outrageous vanity.
Nothing is more common. Writers!—why,
what is the matter with you? Have I
frightened you?"

"Frightened me? No, M. de Tourmagne,"

I cried; but in reality he had startled me
very much.

"Yes," he said, "you looked at me with
such a scared face. It is easy to see you do
not know much about writers. However,
M. Darcet is not one of this description.
Wonderfully as he writes, he is the most
modest of men. He and I have struck up
what I hope may become a true, fast friendship."

"And I know people whom all this will
make very happy."

"Indeed!—and who may they be, pray?"

"Yes, three people: M. Darcet's mother
and sister on his account, and I on yours;
for, besides making a friend, I know what a
pleasure it will be to you to patronize and
eucourage such talents as his."

I now considered that it was high time to
change the conversation; but M. de Tourmagne went on in that little sweet, quiet
manner that you know so well, and that I
love even when it is used to torment me.

"But," he said, "I am not alone in be-
friending the superior merits and talents of
our new author. A lady friend of yours has

of late interested herself very hotly in his welfare. Did you not know it?"

"I beg your pardon?" said I, blushing like a peony.

"Because," he went on, "when I asked some favors of the minister in behalf of M. Darcet, the answer was that they had been already granted at the request of Madame Elise de —— instead of my being, as I thought, first in the desire of being of service to such a promising author."

It was of no use to try and look unconcerned now. My heart was still beating quickly, after the jump it gave at your name, and my color was telling its own tale. M. de Tourmagne saw it and abruptly changed the conversation.

"Favor is the order of the day," he said. "What do you think of M. de Sauveterre's new honors?"

"Not favorable to me," I sighed. "I fear that the new edition to the peerage will prove a great source of unhappiness to me unless you come to my assistance."

"Why, what a strange little creature you are, Stephanie. Do you think that the vis-

oount will not set himself as assiduously as
ever to charm all here?"

"You know my aunt well enough," I replied; "you know M. de Sauveterre and his
mother, and you know what I dread."

He took my hand gently in his own, and
spoke in a way that brought the tears into
my eyes.

"You may add, dear Stephanie," he said,
"that I know enough to be able to reassure
you in all your doubts and fears. Dear
child, you need not dread anything but a
little discussion now and then, and the
necessity of some staunch resistance. You
are too rich, and too lovable also," he said,
stroking my hair softly, "not to attract the
attention of the ambitious De Sauveterres.
Do nothing *brusque* or rash, and confide in
those you love. The ermine of the peerage
may dazzle your aunt's senses for a while,
but it cannot stifle her heart. You deserve
to marry something better than a costume;
and if only embroidery can win you, we
must look out for honors, with a heart under
them. I have a plan in my head——"

"Oh! M. de Tourmagne!" I interrupted,

in a fright, catching his other hand whilst
the tears ran down my cheeks, "help me to
keep my liberty, but do not bring me new
chains. I am very well as I am; do leave
me so."

"Ta, ta, ta," he laughed, breaking away
and making for the door, "a pretty girl of
twenty, rich and good, with a fine character,
well developed, and with no religious vocation, ought certainly to marry. We must
only find a suitable husband, and, if he
comes from China, come he will."

What could he mean, Elise? I hardly
know what to think; but let Madame de
Sauveterre make her appearance now, and I
could meet her bravely, though ten pages in
the Caniac livery held up her most noble
train.

XIX.

JULY 4th.

I had a loving look from Madame Darcet
this morning, and a long chat with Jeanne,
commencing with a kiss. How sweet it is
to be able to make people happy. You know

I always said it was sweeter to give than to receive; though at the present time I can hardly consider that it is all giving and no receiving with me.

"We are all nearly beside ourselves with delight," cried Jeanne, by way of opening a great budget of news. "First of all came a paper the other morning, which of itself had published a long article, which will be of the greatest use to my brother's book. We had scarcely finished reading the article, when an elderly gentleman called to see Germain. Germain was out, and the gentleman waited, speaking in such high terms of the 'Pharaohs' that we were quite delighted. By-and-by, Germain came in; and then how they talked, and looked over books, and discussed so well and so learnedly, and a little warmly, also, until the dinner-bell rang, and our new friend stayed to dine with us. Who do you think he was?—a member of the Academy of Inscriptions, a more valuable acquaintance for Germain to make than a duke and peer, and he would be delighted, he said, to mention my brother's book in the Academy. Well, there is still more to tell.

We really thought wonders would never cease yesterday. I suppose the article in the paper reminded the minister of Germain's petition, for in the afternoon came a message that the royal library would patronize M. Darcet's new book, that the Government would buy two hundred copies of his first, and that the minister desired to see M. Darcet at his earliest convenience. Then the publisher, who had several times sent asking for money, now came to beg the preference for a second edition, which we promised him."

"And what does your brother say to all this?" I asked, smiling.

"He does not know what to think," replied Jeanne, "except that God is very good and very generous to him. My mother and I are half crazy with joy. But, really, we should not wonder at it, for we prayed so much. In confidence: about fifteen days ago the publisher sent for the money which he had advanced for the expenses of printing, etc., and we began a novena, my mother, the servant, and myself, that the book might sell, and the publisher get his money, and

we our peace. God has given us far more
than we asked. I think it is often so. He
is a loving and generous Father."

"A loving and generous Father, indeed,"
I thought, in the depths of my glad heart,
though I was not permitted the relief of
pouring it out like Jeanne. I went to the
church instead, the best place to bring all
our joys and sorrows, and there, as well as
in my own room that night, I thanked God
with tears of gratitude. Does it not seem
like a proof that I am pleasing God in my
present course, when He chooses me actually
to be his instrument in distributing to these
dear ones the very gifts they asked of Him?

XX.

JULY 5th.

Everything has turned out just as I feared.
The Sauveterres are back, higher in my
aunt's favor than ever. They came to visit
this evening, and, oh! dear, how they cajoled
her. I conclude that Madame d'Aubecourt's
wealth is more considerable than I thought,
and that they know better than I do the

breadth and beauty of its dimensions. From
my corner I watched and listened sadly, saying nothing; and the high hopes with which
M. de Tourmagne had inspired me began
little by little to sink and ebb away, until
nothing was left but my courage; it, at least,
is not sinking or ebbing away; quite the contrary. If there was no Germain in the world,
the Sauveterres would still be my horror:
rather a strong word, my dear, but a true
one. I ask you, does it seem right that I
am to be persecuted by these people and
sacrificed to them, just because I am heiress
to wealth which they find necessary to support their selfish grandeur? What would
they care how pretty, or good, or agreeable I
might be; supposing I was all these, as long
as I was merely Captain Corbin's orphan
daughter? And yet, it was precisely when
I was a poor, plain little child, that Germain,
who never heard of Madame d'Aubecourt,
loved me as his sister, watched over me like
a father, and only asked that I should love
him, and develop the good qualities which
he believed he saw springing in my soul to
make me later on his most happy wife.

The viscount made a few attempts to show off and to get me to admire his chatter. I tried to suggest one or two absurdities to him; but he seemed to be on his guard— perhaps his mother had warned him—and I only succeeded in putting him on his mettle; and, oh! dear, my aunt and every one seemed delighted with him. I was in torture.

"Will no one," I thought to myself, "make him feel what a brainless fop he is?"

My charitable wish was soon fulfilled, and I had the exquisite pleasure of seeing the viscount routed by the absent Germain It happened that some one asked where M. de Tourmagne was, and if they should see him that evening.

"I do not think he will be here to-night," I said, "he is dining with a gentleman who has promised to tell him some news about Sesostris."

"Sesostris!" echoed the viscount, "why not Cleopatra? She is the only Egyptian who deserves a memoir."

"*Apropos* of Egypt," said another person, addressing my aunt, "have you read the new book of the day?"

"What new book?" she asked.

"Oh! a book called the 'Pharaohs,' full of Greek and all sorts of hard subjects, and yet so amusing."

"You speak of M. Darcet's book, I presume?" put in another speaker. "Every one is speaking of it. They say that the minister is enchanted with it, and that it is likely to make the author's fortune."

"Have you read it?" asked Madame d'Aubecourt.

You may be sure that I did not answer amongst the many affirmatives to this question. The matter was on the *tapis*, and I was quite content to sit silently watching whilst my victims got meshed in my net.

"Bah!" cried the viscount, as if by instinct, "every one talks about these books whilst they are fashionable. They are a thing of a day, and to-morrow they are forgotten, like the dust of a butterfly's wings. What do you think, mademoiselle?"

"I think," said I, "that the dust will remain when the butterfly is gone."

"Quite so," said the Baroness de V——. "I must beg the pardon of M. le Viscomte, whose wit every one acknowledges; but this book has no need of fashion to make it famous. Every one is amazed to find in so young a writer such extended knowledge, in so learned a writer so much elegance, and in a man of such genius such perfect modesty."

"Add to all this," said my aunt, "that his private life is an example of goodness."

"You know him, then?" cried the baroness. "I should be enchanted if you would introduce him to me."

"I merely know him by seeing him in the church, as yet," was the answer; "but I shall ask M. de Tourmagne to bring him here."

Just then M. de Tourmagne came in, and some one, not the viscount, asked him what was the latest news from the court of Egypt.

"I come," he said, seating himself, "from spending three or four most pleasant hours with a citizen of Memphis." And another eulogy on M. Darcet followed, a eulogy of the subject, not only of his learning, but also of his manners and his goodness. Fancy how delighted I was, especially as M. de Tourmagne has earned a just reputation for being a reader of character.

"You must really bring me this prodigy," said Madame d'Aubecourt.

"If it depended on me," he answered, "you should have seen him here to-night. I was naturally anxious to show such a *man* to the world under my wing. But, unfortunately, he would very much prefer entering into the tent of a Bedouin than into the *salon* of a marchioness. He is too perfect a philosopher not to be a little unsociable."

"People of this class are sometimes wont to hide themselves in the belief that the seldomer seen the more admired," said the viscount, with a sneer.

"There is some truth in that," was the reply; "but others err on the other side, and become wearisome in consequence."

"I must acknowledge," returned M. de Sauveterre, "that I never could see any merit, either real or affected, in this aversion to society."

"It is a fault," said the count, dryly; "but it is the fault of those who have something else to do, and something else to think about."

Bravo! dear M. de Tourmagne. I sat and tasted the sweets of my little revenge, and felt even able to bear the sight of the viscount after seeing this check put upon his best moves, and before my aunt, too. I shall certainly trust to M. de Tourmagne to get me out of my troubles.

What a woman Madame Darcet must be! You see she has faithfully kept her promise of never mentioning my real name to Germain; for if she had not done so, he would never refuse to come here. Contrast this with the conduct of Madame de Sauveterre, who despises me in her heart, and yet plots and plots incessantly to *incorbinate* her proud escutcheon through my wealth. The girl is low-come, and I do not care about her; but she is rich. Caniac to the rescue!

To illustrate a last trait in M. Darcet's wonderful character, M. de Tourmagne related a little fact for the benefit of the whole room, which, I must confess, made my heart beat a little proudly. The minister had offered him a very tempting and very honorable post, and he had refused to accept it, begging his Excellency to transfer his favor to a poor old scholar, who, he said, had more right to it, and deserved it better than he did. My noble Germain!

So there he is—famous. A crowd round him. Every one wanting to know him, and my aunt bent on bringing this new attraction to adorn her *salon.* He will be obliged to come.

But, ah! Elise, what will even the learned, eloquent, illustrious Germain Darcet be in comparison to the Viscount de Sauveterre, heir to the peerage and descendant of the Cauiacs of Perigord?

XXL

JULY 8th.

It is all very well for Germain to be proud and even a little unsociable; but there is a medium in all things;—don't you agree with me, Elise? It is evident that his philosophical and stoical contempt of the world must not be allowed to go the length of preventing him from coming to the Hôtel d'Aubecourt, where every one is so anxious to see him while he is the fashion. It would be a dreadful thing if he were to give offence by his repeated refusals. It struck me that he was badly in want of a little good advice, and so this morning he received the following communication:—"One whom M. Darcet long ago befriended, and whom he has since lost sight of, still remembers the debt of gratitude, and regards it as a duty towards a benefactor to advise him to absent himself no longer from certain *salons*, where he should come in contact with persons having it in their power to exercise a most beneficial influence on his destiny. He cannot be ignorant of the happiness his success would bring his mother and sister, naturally impatient as they are to see him in the high position which his merit deserves. What inconvenience would it be to him to give such and such personages in conversation with him an earlier and better insight into his value and abilities than could be obtained by the perusal of his works? Why should he stand in his own light, and deprive those who love and appreciate him of the sweetness of seeing him in a few years, perhaps in a few months, known and honored as he deserves to be? In the matter of these new acquaintances M. Darcet may safely resign himself to the guidance of M. de Tourmagne.

He will thus avoid a thousand little evils
that his path is strewn with at present. It
is not given to the writer of these lines to
reveal himself to M. Darcet. An humble
and subordinate position forbids it, but it
shall not be always so. Meantime, he begs
M. Darcet to forgive the strangeness of this
advice, and charges him, on his honor, to
mention the matter to no one, not even to
M. de Tourmagne, or to Madame Darcet.
And now, believing that he has done M.
Darcet a real benefit by giving this warning,
he begs in return that M. Darcet will remember him in his prayers. Long ago he
did so, and perhaps he has continued the
practice during our separation. Prayer for
him has become second nature to the writer,
who never did and never will neglect it."

To prevent questions, I directed this note,
not to his own house, but to his publisher's.
When he comes to my aunt's house, shall I
be able to speak to him without making a
fool of myself?

XXII.

JULY 12th.

I was sitting alone in the *salon* last evening; my aunt had laid the wonderful "Pharaohs" on the table and gone up to her own rooms, leaving me to dream away, with my lace work lying in my lap and my needle idle in my fingers. "A penny for your thoughts, Stephanie," cried a laughing voice. I looked up and saw M. de Tourmagne, who had, as usual, entered without being announced; and Germain was with him. He walked in just as he did that day long ago in a dark, hideous garret, and the same Rœschen who thought he brought brightness with him then, rose up trembling and speechless before him in the brilliant *salon*, and thought it, too, was brighter for his presence; and for the first time in eleven years I clasped hands with Germain Darcet. I think I asked him to be seated, and expressed a belief that my aunt was not out; but I fear I was not very intelligible. He looked at me this time with that half-puzzled expression, as if he were trying

to remember where he had seen my face
before. My voice, which, I know, is like
my mother's, seemed to bring back some
confused reminiscences; and I think that
if I had said two or three words in German, he would have called me "Rœschen"
straightway. Yet, how would it ever occur
to him to think of finding in the brilliant, gilded *salon* of the Marchioness d'Aubecourt, the poor little orphan girl whom
he used to take back to the convent in a
fiacre, asleep, with her head on his shoulder.
I said something about telling my aunt,
and left them, glad to have the opportunity of recovering myself. I went first to
my own room, and there I looked in the
glass to judge for myself of what Germain saw when he came into the room : for
at the bottom, you know, I cannot help
wishing him to think me nice. I found
that I was tolerably presentable, tall enough,
slim enough, my German hair, of which he
spoke in complimentary terms of old, being
tolerably arranged and my French eyes none
the worse of the pleasure of seeing him. I
could not help thinking of my old speech,

"Mother, when I am big enough, I will marry Germain," and I laughed to think how true I was to my old sentiments. Then came a reaction. I got frightened at myself, I hardly know why; I threw myself on my knees and said a *Pater* and *Ave*, begging God that I might do His will and not my own. After that I rose quietly and went to look for my aunt.

"Madame d'Aubecourt," cried M. de Tourmagne, as we entered the room together, "allow me to present to you a new *chevalier* whom the king has just created: a *chevalier*, I promise you, '*sans reproche et sans peur.*'" It was then that I saw for the first time that M. Darcet wore in his button-hole the glorious red ribbon; and very becoming it was to his caste, which savors more of the martial than the learned. What a true friend M. de Tourmagne is to me! The conversation was carried on by my aunt, the count, and Germain; for I saw that M. de Tourmagne was doing his very best to turn it to his friend's advantage, and I could resign myself quietly to the pleasure of watching and listening. It was very sweet to see him there

in that gorgeous *salon* which should, please
God, one day be his own, and to listen to his
voice sounding through my thoughts, until
the past seemed to grow soft and sweet and
to rise itself up with the dawning brightness
of the future. My aunt seemed delighted
with him. How entirely he is the opposite
to the Viscount de Sauveterre! He has different ideas, a different accent, a different
class of conversation altogether; and still his
words, though they have a strength and
earnestness which keep you attentive whether
you will or not, possess the most charming
grace and sweetness and gentleness imaginable. I think that if he chose to try
paying compliments and doing the agreeable,
he would manage it much better in his own
natural, vivid way than many whom I have
known to make it their whole study. In
fact, he is something so entirely out of the
common, that when I conjure up the idea
that this wonderful, grave Germain should
one day come to care more for my smiles
than the smiles of glory, that my words
should be of more consequence to him and
give him more to think of than all the

hieroglyphics in the world, that I should hold a higher place in his heart than science, and be next to God in all his hopes and feelings, I grow giddy and feel my plans crumbling, crumbling, and sinking into the impossible. When could my Lord de Sauveterre, with all his honor and all his graces, inspire me with thoughts like these? I felt completely under a charm, and once or twice 1 caught myself, with my needle idle in my fingers and my head bent forward eagerly as I listened to the narratives of his travels, which he was giving my aunt in his interesting way. I shall give you a sample of them. My aunt wished to hear what became of the Christian inhabitants of a certain village of Lebanon, which he had left in a very critical situation, attacked by the Druses.

"On my return," he said, "I found them in greater trouble than ever, and in such a state of alarm that I determined to remain and do what I could for them. Their church had been already pillaged and was sentenced to be burned, and the enemy had carried off a poor young girl away from her father and her betrothed. I was so touched by the old

man's woe and the young man's distraction,
that I went to the Druses to try and induce
them to give up the prisoner. They received
me very badly. I offered a ransom, and it
was refused; I threatened, and they fired on
me. However, their number was not much
greater than ours, and I proposed to the
Christians that we should go and rescue the
girl by force. The people of Lebanon are
very warlike, and my proposition was favor-
ably listened to. Besides my own help I
offered that of my four servants, all brave
and well-armed. We saw that only a bold
stroke was required to get us out of our
difficulties and put a stop to the insults of
the enemy, which were becoming intoler-
able; so my advice, supported by the chiefs,
was accepted at once. We resolved to com-
mence as soon as night was come. Every
one had his arms ready. The priest, who
was in our council, bl·ssed us and heard our
confessions. Two or three men started to
give the alarm to the Catholics of the neighboring villages, and an hour after sunrise
we began the attack. The infidels fought
valiantly, but we were defending our altars,

and God gave us the victory. Besides regaining what they had lost, the Christians secured several important prisoners who would serve as hostages to prevent reprisals, and for whom later on a considerable ransom would be paid."

"And the prisoner—the girl?" asked my aunt.

"We missed her, poor child," replied Germain. "She was not to be found in the house where we believed her to be imprisoned. Her father was too old and infirm to fight, and her lover having been seriously wounded at the first, she was forgotten. Luckily, when we were just about to draw off, two men were seen flying with a woman, whose cries they tried to suffocate. Several of our people started in pursuit, but the Druses were splendidly mounted and were soon far ahead; one Christian, thanks to the swiftness of his horse, succeeded in overtaking them at some distance from the village, and, after a slight combat, rescued the girl."

That was all. But I had a secret conviction that he had more to do with the girl's deliverance than he acknowledged. So I asked a very simple question as to whether this fortunate gentleman happened to be related to the young lady or her lover.

"He was a friend of theirs, mademoiselle," he answered, with a blush.

"The French consul of Beyroot," said M. de Tourmagne, quietly, "who went to the place to settle the quarrel, gives a very detailed account of the affair. The cavalier in question had already done wonders in the combat in the village, and very much simplified matters by killing the chief enemy. He was wounded when he followed in the wake of the young prisoner, and the *slight struggle* by which he delivered her cost him many serious wounds, and ended in the death of the two enemies. On his return, he showed himself a bit of a surgeon by dressing the wounds of the young lady's lover, and never rested until he had cured him and seen them married in the very church which he had so powerfully preserved. I am not at all sure that he did not give away the bride. Altogether the young people might look on him as a valuable friend; eh, Stephanie?"

"I am sure that the Christians of Lebanon

are most deserving," said Madame d'Aubecourt; "but, really, I cannot help feeling
glad that it was a French Catholic who per-
formed such feats as these."

"Also," went on M. de Tourmagne, "in
all Lebanon our hero was called *Roumi-el-
Frank*, which literally means the French
Christian. In Paris, we begin to know him
as M. Germain Darcet."

"Then, indeed, the king did well in giving
him the cross of honor," said my aunt, warmly.

You should have seen M. Darcet's face at
this speech, to which your friend Stephanie
naturally added her little modicum of ap-
plause.

The hero who had killed three Turks in
one evening now grew confused, stammered,
blushed like a school-girl, all to excuse himself for the wondrous doings in Lebanon, and
for the extreme ferocity of the Druses. We
had much difficulty in putting him at his
ease after our burst of admiration, and he
left soon after, having duly promised to come
again. I know that my aunt will very soon
ask him to dine. All this is something
gained, but only something, and for the rest

I must trust to God and to our good old friend the count.

I cannot understand M. de Tourmagne. I can hardly think it possible that he should have formed the same strange, almost hopeless, project as myself; and yet if Germain were his own son he could not take more pride in drawing him out and showing him off than he does. Of course science has drawn them together and united them in affection, and he may never think of me in the matter; but still I think he does think of me all the same.

"What a splendid fellow that is!" said he to Madame d'Aubecourt, when Germain was gone; "he has the material of a statesman in him."

"Yes," said my aunt, "what a pity he is not high-born."

"Well, of course," returned M. de Tourmagne, "but then, most probably, he would not have known so much about the East; and his name, glorious in the past, would never blaze out on the present and the future."

"And what do you expect to make of him, then?" she asked.

"Make of him!" echoed the count; "only a member of the Institute. If I were master, I would like to keep him for science, and leave him to the peaceful happiness of study. But politics will take him up and make him an ambassador or a minister. I should be very glad to see him meet the young Viscount de Sauveterre here and that he should like him."

"Why?" asked Madame d'Aubecourt, in surprise.

"Because," pursued the count, gravely, "M. Darcet might be of very great use to him. In a few years we shall find that M. Darcet's patronage will be a thing worth having."

This glance at the future which showed us M. de Sauveterre, and perhaps his haughty mother, also, in attendance in Germain's anteroom, wounded my aunt's pride, and made me blush up to the roots of my hair. Madame d'Aubecourt saw it, and probably misinterpreted it.

"These are strange times of ours," she said, "when the noblest and most considerable of our old families are continually forced to seek the aid of *parvenus.*"

"Madame de Sauveterre takes the times as they come, you know," said the count; "I should like to know what duke and peer it is whose origin she considers sufficiently irreproachable, or what clerk she has not solicited. And I assure you, she is not alone in this. Every day we see the sons of the people rise up and take the high places, and every day we see the descendants of illustrious houses come to seek the favor of the new-comers, who are there simply because they cannot be done without. It is a great thing, Madame la Marquise, to be a *parvenu*, if we come to gain battles, to defend religion, to govern the State, and to become noble in saving a country. I ask you, which is best —the blood that makes a great man, or the blood that makes a coxcomb?"

"Wise as he is, M. de Tourmagne sometimes puts forward very extravagant opinions," remarked my aunt, when we were alone.

" I think he speaks merely of those who are unworthy of their great name," I answered; "you yourself know how he venerates those who are. When he lauds virtue in this way,

I always think of my grandfather, and cannot help being somewhat of his opinions."

"That is because you are a bit of a Jacobin yourself, my poor child," she said.

"No, dear aunt," I said, "I am nothing; I have not lived as you have through the sad trials which scattered our family. I do not hate, nor can I hate either opinion. You are a royalist; my father was a Jacobin; but I do not trouble myself about people's politics, provided they are good Christians."

"With these ideas," said my aunt, "you will think well of the nobles, and agree that they are necessary to the splendor of States. What do you think of M. de Sauveterre, for instance?" she added, abruptly.

"I do not think anything about him at all, aunt, except that he is a little frivolous," was my reply.

"Bah!" she ejaculated; "he is young."

"Young?" I repeated; "is he not thirty years of age?"

"Well, that's young for a man," she returned. "But perhaps you would prefer the glory of having written a book like this" (and she touched the "Pharaohs," which

lay on the table near her) "to the glory of
bearing a name even so ancient and so beautiful as De Sauveterre?"

"I am no judge of the merits of such a
book as that," I replied; "and it is not my
place to pronounce upon the relative merits
of M. de Sauveterre and M. Darcet; but I
cannot say that I believe Madame Darcet to
have anything to envy Madame de Sauveterre
in point of happiness." There was a silence
for a few moments between us. I knew that
my aunt had something more to say, but I
did not consider it necessary to assist her,
guessing pretty well what it was.

"Do you know," she began at last, "that
you are anything but gracious to M. de
Sauveterre? Do you not like him?"

This thrust caused me to change my tactics: I walked straight on the enemy.

"My own dear aunt," I said, putting my
arms around her neck, "I dislike him only
when I see him succeeding in drawing you
to his side. Believe me, his intention is not
to relieve you of your care of me."

"No," she said; "he would stay."

"Well," I said, "as he wearies me extremely, the less he comes here the happier

I shall be. Let me stay as I am, your loving daughter." The tears were in my eyes, and my aunt was really touched. I saw, with delight, that she would never force me to act against the dictates of my own heart.

"I would like so much to see you happily married," she said after a time.

"I would be glad to marry," I said, "if in so doing I could give you a son in my husband, a loving son, a son full of deference, and respect, and love for so good a mother. One fault I find with M. de Sauveterre, a grave defect, you will allow:—in my opinion, he, as well as his mother, wants heart. He flatters, but he does not love."

"'There, there," said my aunt, "you are not wise, but you are good. We must wait a li tle. Time will dissipate all your prejudices." And I kept silence, satisfied at least to have gained time.

XXIII.

JULY 25th.

It is fifteen days since you heard any news from me, my own dear Elise; meantime everything goes very well for M. Darcet, but very badly for me. Germain has dined here; he has come several times, and my aunt always receives him warmly, especially as he has discovered a knowledge, not of Greek, but, what is far more important, of the heraldry and the history of the old families of France. It was I who discovered this talent: you may be sure I lost no time in setting him to work. He was soon discoursing brilliantly on the subject of genealogy, and recounting how Gervase, the third Màrquis d'Aubecourt, married Bertrande, of the house of Lusignau—a fact unknown before, and the discovery of which raised him to very much esteem. So he goes on, pleasing every one in his simple, unconscious, manly way, and with an easiness of manner which would soon, I fear, be reckoned impertinence if he could be supposed conscious of the unworthy weakness of the young lady of the house. That, however, is not likely. The last-named weakness, which is quite a treason against the mightiness of the D'Aubecourts and the De Sauveterres is securely hidden, and known only to Madame Darcet, who will say nothing. His mother will not tell him, nor M. de Tourmagne, if he suspects anything, as I sometimes think he does. Besides it appears that my love is all in vain. He knows me, he talks to me, he salutes me when we meet, like any other gentleman of my acquaintance, but he does not love me. And to you, at least, I will confess it; I do wish him to love me. I wish him to love me; day and night I pray for the blessing of his love. Perhaps it is selfish; for, if he loved me, what would be gained but the misery to him of crushing back into his heart the love that would seem more hopeless than even it is to me? He would never give me the opportunity to say, "You have looked too high." He would never have it said that he outraged hospitality, and presumed too far. He would never have it said that he was a fortune-hunter, and that he sought the rich inheritance of the Marquise d'Aubecourt. And if he were otherwise than thus proud and sensitive, I should love him less. And yet I want his love. In vain I call upon all the unselfishness of my affection, all the strength of my resolution. There is one point at which my heart is stopped with the cry, "Thus far shalt thou go and no farther." I cannot wish that he should never care for me. A hundred times a day I catch myself with the thought in my mind. I rouse myself from my dream and feel very brave to chase it from my mind, but I soon rush back to it with all the strength of a will that force but half withheld. Then I fancy myself passing through a thousand probable and improbable scenes. Germain would recognize me, and remind me of my childhood, and my childish love for him, and all his generous plans about me, which he had never forgotten. Then how gladly would I resign my right to Madame d'Aubecourt's wealth, and go out with him to share his stormy life as my mother had set me the example. I should no longer be the heiress of a marchioness, but merely Madame Darcet's daughter, Jeanne's sister, Germain's wife, prouder of my place in that happy home than if I sat upon the throne of France. I fancy myself passing across the old court, going up the pretty staircase, with its vine-curtained windows, then a peep into that quiet room with the souvenirs of

my mother and myself, and then away without a word for fear of disturbing Germain,
to sit, needle in hand, between Jeanne and
Madame Durcet, and chat and work the
whole happy, peaceful day. What would I
care for poverty or obscurity, if Germain
loved me, and if my love could bring him
happiness? But then comes the thought of
my aunt. How could I leave her and give
her up? And then, perhaps, Germain himself might be better without me than be
forced to give up his studies, and to work
night and day to support the burden of my
uselessness. No, no, he must not love me,
and be more unhappy than I am myself, and I
will not act in opposition to my aunt's prejudices, and abandon her in her old days. She
has counted on me, and I will never fail her;
but I will try and get her to make a compact
with me, that I will never leave her, and
that she will never force me to marry. And
then Germain will go his way, without
dreaming of Rœschen's existence or the wild
improbability of her loving him, and be
happy as before with his matchless mother
and sister. He has friends now—earnest,

influential friends. He is getting on, and will soon be past the reach of poverty. Perhaps I could not make his life brighter, or more complete. He does not want me. Perhaps he is better without me, so I shall only watch him and pray for him, and wait for another sweet opportunity of being of use to him. If my aunt dies first, and leaves me free, then, before giving to God the willing sacrifice of my remaining life, I shall give my fortune to Germain as a gift from the grateful Rœschen who loved him, and who is dead. When he is rich, his grand soul will expand in the joy of spreading happiness and doing good. Poor fellow! Let Jeanne say what she likes, I can see that he is sometimes very sad. I know too well how to read the folds that weary thoughts leave across the human brow and round the corners of the compressed lips. We read the faces of those we love best, and I read sorrow in Germain Darcet's. My wealth is poverty, my power weakness, when I cannot help him. I would pour out life, and wealth, and happiness at his feet to spare him an hour's pain; and yet there is the puckered brow and the sorrowful mouth, and I cannot raise a finger or speak a word to change them. When I am gone, I shall at least leave him the happiness of doing good.

XXIV.

JULY 30th.

It seems as if I was never, never to be at peace again. Just when I succeeded in calming my thoughts and conquering myself something is sure to occur which will disturb and throw me back further than ever.

The other evening we were strolling in the garden, my aunt, M. de Tourmagne, and myself. Some one, I forget who, mentioned M. Darcet. That gentleman has become a very frequent topic of conversation amongst us, each enjoying it for a different reason: my aunt on account of her love of heraldry, M. de Tourmagne through his craze about Egypt, and I for reasons best known to you.

"*Apropos* of M. Darcet," said my aunt to M. le Comte, "I have a project for him in which I want your help. We must find a nice wife for him."

"Indeed!" cried M. de Tourmagne; "and may I ask whom you propose presenting with such a man as that?"

"Florentine Garby, my solicitor's daughter," was the prompt reply; "Stephanie will tell you all about her. She is a great friend of hers."

"Well, Stephanie, what do you say?" asked M. de Tourmagne, seeing that I took no notice of this remark.

The fact of the matter was that the likelihood of Germain's marrying any one but myself had never presented itself very clearly to my mind, and now it struck me how very possible it was, and how very happily the carrying out of my aunt's project might turn out for both of them. Of course you remember Florentine at school, and know what a dear little thing she is. Well, I have seen a great deal of her since then, and have found her always the same, as gentle and sweet-tempered as she was pretty and attractive. So I steadied my voice, and spoke very nicely on the subject, and in a very calm style, assuring M. de Tourmagne that I was convinced that Florentine would be the very wife for M. Darcet, who had been accustomed to such a charming, gentle sister as Jeanne, whilst the count listened attentively.

"There," cried my aunt, "you see I made a very good choice. Then Garby is rich, a little avaricious with it, perhaps; but he is vain, too, and he is devotedly attached to his daughter. Stephanie shall talk Florentine over to our way of thinking, and I shall dilate to the father on the subject of M. Darcet, Chevalier of the Legion of Honor, who goes to the minister's house, is received in all the best circles, and who is likely, as you say, to become a great man. Stephanie, write and ask Florentine to dine here to-morrow with you and Mademoiselle Darcet; we must bring the two families together."

"Gently, my dear Stephanie," said M. de Tourmagne, very calmly, "do nothing in a hurry; for, I assure you, I do not abandon *my friends* quite so easily, as that." (He laid an accent on the two words and accompanied them by a look which brought the color flashing back into my face.) "In the first place," he went on, "I doubt if M.

Garby, or any other attorney in the world, would give his daughter to a man whose only recommendation was his learning—a recommendation which, I assure you, is not always prized as highly as it ought to be. Secondly, and without denying the attractions of the fair Florentine, I am convinced that even should M. Darcet accept the girl, which is doubtful, he would not accept the dowry. He has certain, very deep-rooted ideas as to the regularity of law-proceedings, and would be anxious to know in how far the property had been accumulated without detriment to the public good. Thirdly, I consider that M. Darcet's wife should be something out of the common. Fourthly, I refuse my consent to the marriage, having other views for my friend. Why, Madame the Marchioness, you have known him a whole month, and can you not see what a brilliant future awaits him?"

"Nonsense, nonsense," cried my aunt, laughingly; "your objections are nothing, my dear count; you cannot expect to get the daughter of a duke and peer for M. Darcet. Florentine is one of his own station in life and would suit exactly. I shall speak to her about it."

"Seriously, do nothing of the kind, madame," said the count, with sudden gravity; "you would disturb the poor girl unnecessarily. I have higher views for my friend, of which he knows nothing, of which I cannot speak just yet, but which I do not wish anticipated."

"Well," said my aunt, "I think you are wrong; let Stephanie be the judge."

"Stephanie," interrupted M. de Tourmagne, "is a dear, good, generous child, whom I love dearly, but I object to accepting her opinion in this matter. If she is of your way of thinking to-day, later on she will most certainly come round to mine."

With this the conversation ended, to my great delight. Soon afterwards I escaped to my own room to think and pray, and I felt very well satisfied with the way in which I had acted. As to M. de Tourmagne, I do not know what to think of him. Has he guessed my secret? Has he really other views for Germain? I feel a great desire to open my heart to him, and then, again, I feel as if I would rather die. It is Stephanie who loves Germain now, not little Rœschen.

XXV.

AUGUST 4th.

Madame Darcet has just given me an account of her success in her efforts, made at my request, to learn something of M. de Tourmagne's probable intentions with regaid to Germain and myself. She went to the *mairie* of the quarter where we lived when my mother died; she there saw the registry of deaths, and found that my mother's decease had been declared by M. de Tourmagne, and by a physician whom I believe to have been Madame d'Aubecourt's own. I suspected that M. de Tourmagne, being my aunt's oldest and most reliable friend, had been taken into her confidence in the matter. And now I am sure that, partly by papers which he saw in my aunt's house, partly in his duty of discharging any little debts which my mother might have left, he has heard something of the noble part which Germain played towards us.

Perhaps he had read, like me, one of his beautiful letters which my aunt may have forgotten. This would account for his recognizing the name of Darcet, when the Curé pronounced it that night in Madame d'Aubecourt's drawing-room. Since then, the "Pharaohs" would probably awaken his memory, and throw a light on the cause of all my efforts to aid my benefactor, and give him a key to my secret. I feel certain that he seconds all my plans.

I cannot but admire the exquisite delicacy, the perfect goodness, and the complete knowledge of my aunt's character that he displays, and then that wicked little way he has of doing good without at all appearing to do it. Madame Darcet thinks as I do. She sees that M. de Tourmagne either knows or suspects something. He is continually asking would-be-careless questions about Germain's past, and one day he managed to draw out the whole history of the painted flowers and the marker. His last move was to beg Germain to promise him that he would never marry without first consulting him. This certainly told a good deal.

"What did Germain answer?" I asked of Madame Darcet, as we walked home from Mass together.

"He laughed, and said he had no intention of marrying. He had already espoused his mother, his sister, and science, and he considered three wives enough for any man."

"How long was this ago?"

"About a fortnight ago."

"Has he always spoken in this way?"

"No," she replied; "and unless I am very much mistaken he would have allowed himself a fourth wife, had he met one he could love. Do you know, dear, though he does not speak much of you, he seems very glad that Jeanne should be a good deal with you."

"I should be very happy if it were God's will that he should love me," I returned; "but in any case I am content, for he seems very happy as he is."

"He always seemed so," said the poor mother, half sadly.

"He never lets me guess at any sorrow he may have. If he has troubles, and I sometimes think he has, he does not tell them to me. Indeed, this is the only fault I have to find with him." The tears were coming up into her kind eyes, and to amuse her, and change the subject, I began to tell her about my aunt's plans for Florentine and my conduct on the occasion.

"My dear child," she said, pressing my hand, "I cannot embrace you in the street; but believe me, I love and bless you with a mother's affection."

We had just reached her door; I bade her good-bye, and flew away as light as a bird. How good she is, and how good M. de Tourmagne is, and how grateful I ought to feel to Providence for having surrounded me with such friends. It sometimes seems to me as if God had set me to walk in a path all closed in and guarded with his best and richest blessings. Ancestors, parents, relations, friends, every one I see, every one I know, every one that touches or belongs to me, good and perfect. They say that life is an arid desert; but there is an oasis flourishing in it, and there I have my happy abode, where everything is fresh and green. Oh, Elise, we dwellers in the oasis must have an awful account to give on the last day; when

we are walking easily in our innocence, our
sisters outside are writhing to resist tempta-
tions; when we are listening with glad ears
to the long-taught lessons of good, their
senses are jarring and tingling to the awful-
ness that has borne down on them from their
birth; we are in the green, shady lanes, fretting against our little crosses, whilst it seems
as if all harm were turned away from our
paths, and they are out in the hot sun, bat-
tling with the guile that has lain on them
from their birth, and surely, surely, "blessed
are they that judge not."

In my sunshine there is only one cloud,
under my flowers there is a serpent, *né*
Caniac, that glides through my garden and
mixes bitterness with my milk and honey;
there is a busy bee of a marchioness hum-
ming about, armed with a sting; but she is
good, and the sting will by-and by be turned
against the serpent; and then there will be
nothing more to do but to sit down quietly
in the shade and decipher our hieroglyphics,
giving thanks to God: that is, when the serpent is chased out, and the bee induced to
change her tactics.

XXVI.

AUGUST 10th.

My dear Elise, I am very happy, and I am very sad. He loves mè, and he wants to go away! He loves me! He has not told me so, but I know it. I have seen him jealous, sad, and reassured by a word of mine, passing from sorrow to joy in a few hours, on my account, altogether on my account. I do not think it is very hard to guess at, and feel pretty sure, whether a person loves you or not, without requiring any very wonderful proof. I first began to have my suspicions when I perceived that Germain, who is so completely at his ease with every one else, was awkward and half shy when he spoke a word to me. One day he gave me his arm going into dinner; he trembled, and I had some difficulty in restoring his composure. Another day we were all strolling about in the garden; I plucked a few flowers and made a little bouquet, which I afterwards forgot on a seat. They disappeared; and a few minutes afterwards, Germain, in taking some papers out of his pocket to give to

M. de Tourmagne, drew out my bouquet,
which I recognized at once, though my
Maronite hid it again. with some haste.   I
understand these little traits very well.   I
tremble, too, when I take his arm; and side
by side with my precious letter I have hidden
a little sprig of mignonette which he that
evening gathered.   Of late his awkwardness
in speaking to me is wearing off; and now
he talks freely about his adventures and tells
me his thoughts and ideas, on different subjects: perhaps because he feels instinctively
that I take pleasure in hearing him, that I
take an interest in them, and then the exquisite refinement of his mind-finds a ready
response in mine.   Generally he talks to my
aunt when he is here; but something tells
me that he means it all for me.   Last night
my suspicions became certainties.   And last
night, I heard that he means to go away
again.   He dined with us ; and as it was my
aunt's birthday, others came in the evening,
amongst whom was Madame R——.   She
was, of course, asked to give us some music;
she took it into her head to play a quadrille,
and a sort of little dance was improvised.

M. de Sauveterre at once engaged me, whilst
Germain watched attentively. I was very
happy; I am always happy when Germain is
there. M. de Sauveterre said witty things;
I laughingly returned his sallies, and we
were just getting on a great deal better than
usual, when my eye was caught by a little
tableau opposite us. Germain was bending
over an old friend of my aunt's, an inveterate
talker. She was chattering away whilst Germain listened with a troubled, earnest face,
his eyes all the while fixed on M. de Sauveterre and myself. I knew very well what
she was telling him when I saw them; for of
late, partly through my aunt, partly through
my foppish admirer himself, and partly
through that arch-conspirator, Madame de
Sauveterre, the report has got about that we
are engaged. Why, I fancied I could read
in Germain's darkening face every word that
most good-natured but most loquacious of
women was saying. She was holding forth
on the subject of my dowry and my approaching brilliant marriage. Poor fellow! how
sorrowful he looked, though he tried hard
to control it. Perhaps it was only then that

he himself realized how he loved me, and
how improbable it was that he should win
me. For, putting my feelings out of the
question, he knows very well the opinions my
aunt holds as to rank, and I have seen him
wince over and over again, though she, excellent creature, would never see it. Then
it struck me that Germain would most certainly read M. de Sauveterre's character at a
glance, and then how could he help feeling
a little contempt on hearing what he did
just now. The idea changed my tone and
humor very quickly. In a moment M. de
Sauveterre's witticisms were unnoticed; my
mind was full of one thought of how I could
win back M. Darcet's good opinion. I
forgot that I was Madame d'Aubecourt's
heiress; the shadow of the armories of
D'Aubecourt and De Sauveterre was lifted
from my spirit, and I was only little Rosalie
Corbin, fretting that M. Germain was dis-
pleased with her. If he comes to think that
he has been mistaken in the nobleness and
refinement of my mind and heart, at once
he will cease to care for me, and I shall lose
him.

While I was wrapt in these thoughts the
viscount chattered away, but got no answer.
He complained at last and bewailed his mis-
fortune. He reminds me of people in come-
dies who come to pierce their hearts at the
feet of an ingrate; how quietly I could say,
"pierce, by all means." But as he has no
sword, and it is a weapon for which, I fancy,
he has no particular predilection, I may make
my mind easy. Forgive me, O most charitable Elise; for, really, when I think how he
threatens to spoil my life, as he has already
half spoiled my heart, I lose all patience.
He and his mother alone have given me all
those hard, bitter feelings which you condemn in me. Germain had left off watching
us, and was standing in a corner with M. de
Tourmagne. The count seemed to be speaking hotly, about something, while Germain
listened with a calm, almost obstinate air.
What could be the matter? A sort of pre-
sentiment of coming ill seemed to sink down
and settle like a cloud upon my heart. I
wished that Germain would at least look
over again; but no; you would think he had
made a compact with his eyes, so persistently

did he keep them fixed on the ground without stirring a lid.

The quadrille over, the viscount took me back to my place. I could hardly contain myself, I felt so put out. Madame de Sauveterre bent forward and asked me if I felt ill. Poor Madame de Sauveterre, can she never lose any opportunity of making me dislike her? I fancied she was spying on me, and I felt indignant at her pretended interest. Oh! I must take care, for sometimes I think and act in anything but a Christian manner. I answered shortly that I was quite well; and then, without caring what she thought, and to show her that I was quite well, I got up and went straight over to the spot where M. de Tourmagne was still talking to Germain, not exactly knowing what I was going to do, or what I was going to say. They were so entirely absorbed in their conversation that neither saw me approach.

"It is folly," M de Tourmagne was saying very emphatically; "utter folly."

"But it must be done," answered Germain, sadly and firmly.

I was quite close to them. Germain jumped

up, looking very much put out, and M. de Tourmagne looked at me with an expression half of annoyance and half of bewilderment.

You are going to find me quite mistress of myself, my dear Elise, and perhaps, too, a bit of a dissembler; for I had sufficient control over myself to look quite unconcerned and say smilingly: "If it is a question of the 'Pharaohs,' which is under discussion, I shall plead ignorance and withdraw."

"Yes," replied M. de Tourmagne, still with his brows knit. "It is a question of the 'Pharaohs'—confound them for all the follies that they lead sensible men into. Here is M. Darcet wanting to start off after them again. If you have charity, Stephanie, pray that he may come to his senses."

"I assure you," said poor Germain, with a smile that went to my heart, "the more I listen to reason the more I see that I must go."

"But what will your mother and sister say, M. Darcet?" I cried.

"Thanks to the minister and all the good friends I have found," replied Germain. "My mother and sister do not want me; they will go into a convent, and be quite happy."

"Happy!" I echoed; "happy, and you so far away, in the middle of yellow fever, perhaps!"

"Yellow fever is an old acquaintance of mine," he said; "and there are other fevers in Paris to which I am less accustomed. I must go back to my desert."

"Folly," repeated M. de Tourmagne; "folly, even if it were the folly of learning."

"And such it is," put in Germain.

"No, no," cried the count, "it is the folly of a very young man. Do not fancy that I will help you to its accomplishment; there is not the slightest necessity for your going back to Egypt."

"Provided I leave Paris," said Germain, "it is all the same to me where I go. I have something to do in Bengal, and then I may make a regular tour round the world."

"It is Paris that you find fault with, then?" I said.

"It is Paris that I find fault with," he answered; "I can do nothing of any value here, and I am likely to fall into misanthropy; so, M. de Tourmagne, I beg that you will see the minister to-morrow."

"Be perfectly certain that I shall do nothing of the sort," said the count; "and, moreover, I shall do all in my power to oppose you.".

"Mademoiselle," cried Germain, "I beg you to use your influence with M. de Tourmagne in my behalf."

"Why, what would Madame Darcet say to me?" I laughed. "Oh, no, you must not count on me."

There was a quadrille forming just at that moment. I was not engaged, and I saw that another couple was wanting to complete the figure. Not seeing a pair to fill the place, I turned to Germain, and asked him to join it with me, gaily excusing myself on the plea that it was part of my duty to see after the pleasure of our guests.

"In all Paris you would hardly find a worse dancer," he said, as we took our places.

"And this accident will probably make you more than ever in a hurry to leave us?" I said.

"I would answer yes," he said, "if I could explain my meaning."

"And why can you not explain?" I asked.

"Do not ask me; it would be a dissertation," he said.

"Indeed," I went on, "I do not wonder at any one hating the world."

"But I do not hate the world," said Germain. "Only things do not always go just as I would wish to see them; and when I can do nothing, I would rather go away from the sight that saddens me."

"And you go away without regret?" I asked.

"No," he replied; "I go away without hatred. Perhaps it is I who am mistaken and the world that is reasonable. We judge differently, that is all."

Neither of us mentioned M. de Sauveterre's name; but the figure and false glitter of my noble admirer was at the bottom of our conversation, and we both felt it. I drew Germain on with my questions; he tried to evade me for awhile, but I knew that in the end he was glad to tell me some of his thoughts.

"And in what do you differ from the world?" I persisted.

"On many, many points."

"I should like to know some of them."

"But I cannot tell you," he cried; "I do not want to leave you with a bad impression of my taste, and I fear that my antipathies would be at variance with your sympathies."

"So you think you know my sympathies?" I returned; "but, I assure you, monsieur, you are mistaken; and I, who know your antipathies, assure you that they do not jar on me in the least. No," I went on, as he looked at me in surprise; "I have no taste for the tinsel and hollow glitter which I know you despise. I never loved the frivolity we see around us, never for one instant was I dazzled or charmed by its eternal whirl and prattle, and the patience which I show with all this comes at times, less from the spirit of submission to the world than from the secret contempt which I have for it."

"I am very happy to hear you say so," cried Germain; "and, may I add, that I have always suspected as much. But I think you are the only one here who feels in this way."

"Well," I said, a little stiffly, "and is that nothing?"

"It is everything," he murmured, "everything."

I went on without pretending to hear him: "But I am not the only one here who feels in this way. Without speaking of M. de Tourmagne, whom you will hardly accuse of overlooking real merit, there are many around us, with my aunt at the head, who would, were the question seriously put to them, acknowledge that they are very little deceived by this outward brilliancy. It draws a smile from them, often a smile of compassion; but their hearts, their sympathies, their esteem, they reserve for the good and true. The world is not as silly as you think."

"And I," said Germain, "do not think it as silly as you believe I do. The false spirit of which we have spoken is like the moss growing on the rocks: under the moss is a solid substance called name, position, anything you like; to this the world tenders its esteem, authorized, I know, by very powerful reasons. In a word, they believe that they can build a future on a mere ancient name, as men build a strong castle on a sterile rock."

That night, when I went up stairs, I opened the window of my boudoir—the one that overhangs the garden—and sat down to think, on the cushioned seat where you and I spent so long, one night, chatting happily about your approaching marriage. The bright stars peeped out, and wafts of balmy air came up from the quiet garden. All seemed so calm that I half wondered at my own restlessness, and things began to get dim and dreamlike. How sad the future looked. I might see that garden change and rechange, the limes drop their leaves and bud again, the fragrant mignonette come and go, before my sad soul should have won back, not its lost hopes, but even peace itself, or have even grown used to sorrow. Until then, no scene, no matter how beautiful, or peaceful, or sweet, could console me. Can it be that God would condemn us to such ceaseless sorrow? Oh, no, I would not say that. In the greatest sorrow which Providence sends us we shall find good; and God always pours balm into a suffering soul. If I did my duty, I told myself, God would work out his wonderful designs, and never forsake me. Over the ruins of my dearest hopes I would walk confidently, knowing that the divine help is never refused to us in our misfortunes. I would smile as my dying father smiled; for I am come of a race that never forsook its God in sorrow.

XXVII.

AUGUST 15th.

You must pray for me, my own Elise, I am in dire want of prayers, for I am at the very turning-point of my life, and my courage, which a fortnight ago I thought so high, is now sinking little by little, just when I have most need of it. Since my last letter I have seen neither Germain nor Madame Darcet, and Jeanne knows nothing. I have, however, had a talk with M. de Tourmagne, which, I think, will interest you.

"My poor child," he began, "I want to put you on your guard about something. The De Sauveterres, for whom, I fear, you have no great love, are becoming more dangerous than I expected. The countess has managed to work her way to the Dauphiness.

She has quite enough of tact to win the favor of the good princess, and quite enough cleverness to know how to interest her in her plans."

"Oh, M. de Tourmagne!" was all I could say.

"My authority is only too good," he went on; "you must be on your watch for every stroke from this point. As long as M. de Sauveterre had only your aunt and his mother to back him up, the matter was really in your own hands, to accept or to refuse. But if her Royal Highness draws your aunt aside some fine day and tells her that she wishes you to marry the Viscount de Sauveterre, she can never refuse her, and nothing will be left to you but obedience."

"Oh, M. de Tourmagne!" I cried passionately, "they little know me. I'll never obey;—I'd rather die at once."

"I quite believe that," returned the count; "but, perhaps, it would be better neither to obey nor to die; and it would be better, if possible, to spare your kind aunt the annoyance of giving unpleasant explanations to her Royal Highness. Is there no means of

foreseeing and arranging all this without
noise or trouble?"

"I do not know of any," I answered, in
tears, fairly beaten by this new trouble.

"Come now," urged M. de Tourmagne,
"just think it over; and, above all, don't
cry about it. Suppose, for instance, that
you had, a little slily, but still with due
reason and consideration, chosen for yourself,
and that Madame d'Aubecourt could, at her
next visit to the Tuilleries, announce your
approaching marriage; do you think any
one would even hint at the viscount? Not
at all; there would not be a word about him."

He took my hand and looked down into
my face questioningly. There I stood before
him, trembling and silent. He had certainly
done his best to put me at my ease and to
invite my confidence. I drew away my hand
and pressed it tightly in the other; but I
could not speak. Germain's name died away
unspoken. I could not mention him to this
man, who knows, and loves, and appreciates
him so. How, then, shall I speak of him to
my much-prejudiced aunt?

"After Madame d'Aubecourt has been informed of the state of your feelings," he went on, "some friend, whom I think we shall manage to find, could, if necessary, talk her round to understand your reasons and ideas, the impossibility of forcing you, and the necessity of having an answer ready for the viscount. We might even point out to her how the De Sauveterres had been obliged to resort to royal authority to carry you off. I think I can undertake to make this point pretty clear to her."

"And could you not make the others clear to her, also, M. de Tourmagne?" I pleaded.

"No, no," was the answer; "for the very reason that I should not, nor do I wish to, know anything before Madame d'Aubecourt does; the ice must be broken by you; besides, there might be things to be said which would be better kept between yourselves; nor have I your eloquence. Come, my child, courage, courage! Ask yourself if your mother would have approved of all you are doing, and then do bravely what she would have sanctioned. Be perfectly certain she would not have given you to the Viscount de Sauveterre. I have heard much about her lately *from one*

who knew her well. She must have been a
most generous and a most holy woman; and
I am sure she is praying for you now in
heaven."

"God bless you for saying so, dear M. de
Tourmagne," I said, "and God bless you for
all your goodness to me."

"My child," he said, very tenderly, "you
deserve to be happy, and happy you shall
be; and that happiness shall be the last and
greatest joy of my life;—but that is enough
about it," he added, abruptly; "it is all
settled. You shall have your chat with your
aunt to-day, or to-morrow, the sooner the
better; and, meantime, I am very sad on my
own account. Darcet, whom I love as if he
was my own son, insists on making a new
voyage. He wants to go to discover Ninive;
—a fine project, no doubt, but somewhat
inopportune. He has already applied to the
minister for a mission to the countries of the
Levant, and I do not know how to keep him."

"But he is not going just yet, is he?" I
asked, tremblingly.

"Why, in fifteen days from this he is to
be at his chosen post. Meantime, I do not

despair of keeping him in Paris and embarking him in other and happier pursuits, of which I have not as yet spoken to him. I think that, like you, he has a special saint protecting him from heaven, a real saint, whose aid I might invoke for him with great confidence. Do you know that Mademoiselle Joyant was his relation and godmother?"

"What!" I cried; "Mademoiselle Joyant of Laval?"

"Precisely. I heard it yesterday by accident. You are not ignorant of the great services which Mademoiselle Joyant has rendered to your family? Remember this if there is ever any necessity to raise my friend Germain in Madame d'Aubecourt's good graces."

Having tendered me this new argument, of which I intend to make good use, the dear, good count went away, and I flew up here to write to you, whilst I was waiting for my aunt to come in from her drive. I should like to speak at once; for, besides the loss of time, I should only be tempted to put it off too long if I waited for a more favorable occasion than the present, and I mean to be very brave.

She is coming, Elise; I hear her carriage;
I dare not think of what I am going to do
for fear I should give up.

XXVIII.
August 16th.

I have gone through a great deal since I
wrote to you yesterday morning, and now
you are going to hear the end of my story.
I said a very fervent prayer, and then went
down to meet my aunt with a firm step, but
a very troubled face. I saw at once that
she was in a bad humor, which did not tend
to reassure me.

"Good gracious! Stephanie," she cried,
the moment I appeared, "what on earth is
the matter with you? Such a face! Are
you ill?"

"No, aunt, there is nothing particular the
matter with me," I said; "I have a little
headache, that's all."

"You seem to have a succession of head-
aches now-a-days," she returned; "you are
not yourself; you are sad, absent, dreamy.
One would think, to look at you, that you

were the most unhappy creature in Paris.
Such airs do not become a girl like you, by
any means."

I felt very much inclined to cry, but I
checked myself. Madame d'Aubecourt does
not like any one to cry when she scolds.
"Forgive me, dear aunt," I said, with a
great effort, "and listen to me; for I want"—

The Viscount de Sauveterre was announced. For the first time in my life I
was glad to see him. He came in scarcely
seeming to touch the carpet, fresh and
smiling as Aurora, most faultlessly dressed,
showing his white teeth, and evidently enchanted with the world in general, and
Madame de Sauveterre in particular, dress,
figure and all. He kissed my aunt's hand,
made me a gallant, lingering bow, and then
sat down with an air which said plainly,
"Here I am, charming, handsome, high-
born!—feast your eyes upon me." My aunt
received him complacently. He had, as
usual, a budget of news, which he began to
unfold with little bursts of laughter, little
grimaces, and all his pretty, foppish tricks.
Very soon Madame d'Aubecourt began to

forget her bad humor—a fact which I was
very sorry to observe. I would rather she
should remain vexed, and scold me ever so
badly, if only the viscount came in for a
stroke or two. However, he said no word
that could displease her, but, on the contrary, pleased and flattered her perfectly.
When the viscount is merely a fop, I dislike
him; but when I see him getting on well
and cleverly, I cannot endure him. And he
was getting on splendidly yesterday morning. He began to tell how Madame la
Dauphine complained that Madame d'Aubecourt had neglected her for some time past.
This was pure invention, of course; but my
aunt swallowed it; for though she assiduously cultivates the favor of the princess,
she would fain appear to care nothing about
it. Those De Sauveterres know her well.
She became more and more amiable to her
visitor. "Tell me," she said, "when does
your father make his first speech in the
House?"

"As soon as I have it ready," was the
reply.

"Good! What do you mean to speak of?"

"Well, I had some excellent considerations to urge against the present shape of hats, which I consider frightful; but my father wished to speak of finances."

"How strange!" cried my aunt, laughing outright;—"and how will you manage about it?"

"Perfectly," said the viscount; "the speech will be made without my losing even one hunting-party. Then, I assure you, my father has some very good things to say. The Opposition affirms that two-and-two are three at the utmost, and we will prove that two-and-two are five at the least."

By means of all this prattle the viscount gave my aunt to understand that he was no longer a Jacobin, and that he was occupying himself with very serious affairs. He succeeded. I felt myself getting so unhappy that I was again inclined to cry. I longed for some one to come in; I was mentally speculating on the probability of M. de Tourmagne returning when Germain walked in. What a contrast there was between him and the viscount. It seemed as if I had never known the breadth and the depth of the

difference between them until this, perhaps
the last opportunity I should ever have of
comparing or choosing between them.
Though nearly of the same height, Germain
looks a full head taller; but even with his
sunburnt forehead, his grave manner, and
his quiet words, dropping here and there,
just where they are wanted, like ripe wall
fruit, Germain seems the younger. There is
something battered and worn-out about the
viscount's gaiety when you see him beside
my hero. It is the forced hot-house plant
beside the vigorous tree of the open air; or,
if you like it better, the spaniel by the side
of the proud lion. Ah! my handsome viscount, most valiant hunter of hares! if you,
though already wounded, had started off in
pursuit of two fully armed Druses, who
were carrying a poor girl away to their den,
what a charming boast it would have been
to tell! The calm Germain is full of enthusiasm; the restless viscount has nothing
in his brains but chatter and raillery. The
veriest butterfly that passes him is not be-
neath his notice; he gambols, he sparkles, he
is pliant, graceful, charming; Germain is

unmoved. But see him when some grand idea is put forward, when the history of some noble action is recounted: see him when there is question of religion, or politics, or arts, or of the sufferings of the poor; then he speaks. The warm glow spreads over his grand face, his soul wakes up, and his voice, that calm, quiet voice of his, rolls and softens again, and trembles lightly at times, till every one feels his subject, every one except the viscount; he holds his tongue, evidently very much bored; for he is never happy except when he is chattering himself; you can see it in his face, in his restless eyes and knitted brow; he frets and fidgets until he gets the public gaze on himself once more.

Germain is amongst the few people whom my aunt treats with neither patronage nor *hauteur*, in fact, as if they were something out of the common. His very look forbids impertinence of any kind. The viscount himself loads him with civility; it would never do for his future *Seigneurie* to let it be thought he had stooped to be jealous of plain M. Darcet the writer. Had I not known what was passing in Germain's heart, his

face would have told me nothing yesterday.
You could catch a sad shade on his face as
he looked from one to the other of us, that
was all; but in this I thought I read the
confirmation of my dread, the assurance that
his sacrifice was complete, and that he was
indeed going to leave us. Soon after he
came into the room my aunt asked him how
soon he intended starting on his journey,
and he answered that he had come to bid us
good-bye. I heard him say it; but I never
changed countenance; I only looked over at
him; and when I saw his eyes fixed on the
ground, I knew he was avoiding me. It was
evident that he had never guessed at my
feelings for him; so I felt touched at his
determination, and I thought how astonished
he would be if, perhaps, at some distant day,
he were to learn how I had loved him. The
viscount asked him where he meant to go,
and he answered:

"To the East, as far away as I can go."

"I cannot imagine what people want that
they fly off to these savage places," was the
flippant rejoinder.

"I want many things, which I hope to
find there," said Germain, gently.

"But I always do and always will wonder why people cannot find everything they want in Paris. Search about a bit, and I fancy you will find every imaginable thing, even the plague itself."

"Or something analogous," laughed Germain; "but it is not exactly the plague that I want. The Eastern sky is beautiful, and the Eastern countries full of instruction. They are the countries that I love, and I did not find them so savage as you seem to think them. I spent happy and peaceful days there with good people and good stones, which told me more than all the books in the world."

"That does not tempt you much, viscount?" said the marchioness.

"No, madame," was the gallant reply; "my bright days and my happiness are here. I know of nothing more instructive or more attractive than the commerce of the world, the hurry of business, and the charms of art. Unless I am sent off some day as an ambassador I shall never go far beyond the quays and the opera."

"Our roads lie in opposite directions,"

Germain remarked, "and we shall both, I hope, follow his own faithfully, one in the elegant chateau, the other in the tent of the traveler."

"I think," said Madame d'Aubecourt, "that after traveling for awhile the tent should be pitched and become a home. Seriously, M. Darcet," she went on, "do you not think that a nice quiet house, well furnished with old books, brightened by the faces of a loving wife and pretty children would be preferable to the fairest sky and the most wonderful stones in Asia? In my idea, when stones begin to build up a wall between you and happiness, they are fast forming a prison of science."

This little tableau seemed to take Germain completely by surprise, as indeed it did me.

"Madame," he said hurriedly, "I am a traveler, and on my way I have sometimes looked into the homes of those who live happy lives among their children, and the thought has arisen that I, too, would be glad to rest so; but God does not wish it, and I go my way, trying not to murmur. You know we do not always find happiness just

where we expected it. The thing we long
for deceives us and it would be ungrateful
to murmur."

"For instance," cried the viscount, "for
instance"—he stopped short. I do believe
he had spoken from sheer longing to speak
and hear the sound of his own voice once
more.

"I had a godmother," went on Germain,
quite taken up with thoughts which he appeared unable to restrain, "a relation of
mine, and a most pious creature; her life had
been thrown in the most terrible and extraordinary adventures; and she used to say
that she never in all her life saw any person
bowed down by trial that it did not turn out
to be the very interest of their soul. I
believe it to be so."

When Germain mentioned his godmother,
I thought I was all right, and I hastened to
avail myself of the opportunity. "Monsieur," I said, "that is certainly a maxim I
should like to bear in mind. May I ask
what was your godmother's name?"

"She left the reputation of a saint behind
her in our country," he answered; "she was
called Mademoiselle Joyant."

I thought that the name of Mademoiselle
Joyant would have worked wonders and
drawn down on her fortunate godson the
very sunshine of Madame d'Aubecourt's
favor. What was my disgust to see her
perfectly unmoved, as if the presence of that
wretched fop of a viscount had frozen her
heart. The Marchioness d'Aubecourt dared
not show herself as the daughter of old
Corbin, and all I got for my little *ruse* was
a vexed look that chilled my heart. "My
God," I thought, "what can be hoped from
such pride as this!"

For two whole minutes the viscount had
held his peace; so, considering it was high
time to re-enter on the scene, he said a few
sparkling things and then begged Germain
to send him the costume of a Janissary, ad-
vising me to take this opportunity of pro-
curing the dress of a Greek girl for the next
fancy ball. I thanked him very dryly for
his advice, assuring him that I had no particular taste for fancy dress. He bowed,
and responded with some witticism, which I
threw back to him scornfully. But nothing
could disconcert him; and Madame d'Aube-

court threw herself into the breach, as she always does when the viscount is getting the worst of it. "Do you know, monsieur," she said to Germain, "that you have more the appearance of resignation than contentment? To tell you the truth, I am astonished at your undertaking this new voyage."

"It certainly costs me something to go, madame," he answered; "I thought my wanderings were over, but I find that I must go."

"Paris will avenge herself," put in the viscount, "by the sharpness of your regret, before you are very long away, M. Darcet."

"I am afraid that you do me too much honor, monsieur," said Germain, smiling. "Most of the things that I will regret would probably appear to you very insignificant. I regret neither commerce, nor quays, nor opera, but only my lamp and my little corner at home. I could be very happy with my mother and sister."

"Oh!" interrupted my aunt, "I forgot about them for the moment. What do they say to this sudden idea of yours?"

Germain's face changed. His courage,

which had been gradually diminishing, seemed suddenly to forsake him altogether.

"Madame," he said, in a tone which no one but the viscount could listen to unmoved, "I have not dared to tell them yet. You may judge what a grave reason I have for going when it has determined me to give them such a trial."

The words were so simple, and yet so sad, that they cut straight to my heart. I felt that if I stopped any longer I should betray myself; accordingly, I started up, the tears gathering thick in my eyes, and left the *salon,* to cry it out in my own room. Neither Germain nor the viscount remarked it; but my aunt did, and I caught a look as I was disappearing which tended very much to increase my alarm. I felt literally done up with sorrow and fear. How would Madame d'Aubecourt ever bend? Why, why had I plotted only to bring my dear friends into the anguish of this separation? It was all over. I could never be happy again, for I had dragged others down who were dearer far than myself. I saw no way out, no faintest glimmering of hope, no courage, no resignation, nothing but desolation. It is a terrible thing to stand after the battle vanquished, ruined, disarmed, and with the blighted happiness of our fellow-creatures lying at our guilty feet. "Oh, misery!" I sobbed, "why, why did I not tell all at first? Why did I plot, and plan, and make him love me! God is punishing me now, by refusing me the happiness that I tried to win for myself, but which I was unworthy of winning!" For about half an hour I lay with my face buried in my pillows, hugging my sorrow and sobbing over it, when suddenly I felt that there was some one in the room, and I started up to find myself face to face with my aunt who was watching me sternly.

Poor, dear aunt, how falsely I judged her! The severity did not last long; and then she sat down near me, and taking my hands, said two words, two gentle words, that won me to her forever and turned the very tide of my fate.

"Stephanie," she said "confide in me, child."

I required no second bidding. In an instant my arms were round her, and my long-shut-up heart poured out all its sorrows on her breast. Nothing was kept back. The misery of my childish days, Germain's goodness, the letter from Naples, the visit to Madame Darcet, everything that I have told you. I saw how deeply she was moved at parts of the story, and I saw that Germain held a very high place in her heart. She never asked, however, why it was that I had not confided in her before; we both felt the reason and neither touched on it. In a word, I thought I saw that Corbin, feeling humbled by the triumph of D'Aubecourt in the matter of Mademoiselle Joyant, was prepared to avenge itself on her generous heart; but I would not expect too much. "And now dear aunt," I said, "you know all; I beg you to forgive me, and I ask but one favor; do not force me to marry M. de Sauveterre."

"You are a little fool," she interrupted, kissing me; "bathe those red eyes of yours with cold water, rest yourself awhile, and, in future, do not doubt your mother's love."

Then she left me, and I did not see her until dinner, which was the strangest meal I ever was at. My aunt looked fidgety, excited, and happy. M. de Tourmagne, who was our only guest, looked frankly and perfectly enchanted. There was nothing left for me to think but that something very good had happened or was going to happen. I had, of course, no idea of what was coming; but whether it was the relief induced by my burst of confidence, or that the gaiety of the other two was infectious, I felt on the very point of crying for joy, and was inclined to jump up and kiss my aunt, or dance round the room, or show some other extraordinary symptom of exuberant spirits.

We were scarcely seated in the *salon* after dinner, when a servant came in, and, stepping up to my aunt with a wonderful air of mystery, said two words in her ear.

"Very well," said my aunt, "do what I told you." Then she turned to me with dancing eyes, crying:

"Quick! quick! Stephanie, hide yourself!"

"Hide myself!" I echoed, in amazement.

"Hide yourself, you little goose," she repeated, half-pushing, half-leading me into her own room, which opened off the *salon*. I was hardly inside the door when I heard the servant announce M. Darcet.

"Not a word," cried my aunt, with her finger on her lip, laughing merrily at my wonder-stricken face. "I am going to receive him and have a little talk with him; but I do not altogether forbid people listening at doors."

One more kiss, and then away she went as gaily as you yourself could have gone if you were in her place. I lost no time in taking her hint, and watching and listening through the half-open door.

"M. Darcet," she began, solemnly, "I have sent for you to speak on a very important subject, which M. de Tourmagne and I have already considered. You must know that my family is under great obligations to you."

"To me, Madame d'Aubecourt?"

"To you, and to one of your relations. Firstly, Mademoiselle Joyant of Laval gave the most blessed comfort that could be given to my father and mother when they were doomed to the death of the scaffold in 1793. After their death, with still more courageous devotion she hid me, their daughter, and so saved my life."

"Madame la Marquise is from Laval," observed M. de Tourmagne.

"But that is not all," continued my aunt, enjoying the utter amazement of Germain's face. "My niece, Stephanie, has discovered that before your first journey, ten years ago, you helped a relation of mine out of the most awful ditsress. This relation, whom I did not then know, was an officer's widow, called Madame Corbin."

"Madame Corbin!" echoed Germain in a tone that thrilled to my very heart." "Oh, Madame la Marquise, do tell me what has become of little Rosalie."

"Little Rosalie is quite grown up now," she said, smiling. "I think you would hardly recognize her. We shall speak of her later on; meantime, to the important subject. In what I am going to say you must excuse me, on the plea of the unbounded interest which gratitude forces me to take in you and yours. You are intending to take a voyage, which will cause agony to your poor mother, which will be long, perilous, and, if we are to believe M. de Tourmagne, useless."

"Useless! unreasonable! senseless!" cried

M. de Tourmagne, letting off every word like
a shot at Germain's head.

"Let me finish, please, M. Darcet," said
Madame d'Aubecourt, as Germain essayed to
defend himself against the shots, "let me
finish, and then you shall give us your objections. We, your friends, M. de Tourmagne, my niece, and myself, have resolved
to try and prevent you from taking this
step. Now, give me your whole attention
while I put before you an idea which has
been in my mind for some time, but which
was impressed anew upon me this morning
by my niece, Stephanie; for, you know,
Stephanie loves your mother and sister very
much, and is very much interested; and I
hope that our plan will not be unacceptable
to you. I think it will not. Don't you, M.
le Comte?" she added, laughingly, to M. de
Tourmagne.

"It should not, madame," was the grave
reply, "for the idea is worthy of you."

"Well, then, *dear M. Germain*," she wound
up, with a little emotion, "we want you to
marry."

I started as if I had been shot at this last

word. I was bewildered, astounded; and for some moments the voices in the other room, even Germain's own, sounded far away, and I did not hear what they said. Then I threw myself on my knees at the prie-dieu before Madame d'Aubecourt's altar to pray. I lifted my eyes and saw, instead of the beautiful ivory crucifix that generally hangs there, an old crucifix of bronze. I knew it at the first glance after ten long years, the very one on which my dying father had gazed, the very one to kiss which Germain had lifted me up that morning when he told me that here was my one true protector and friend. And it was at these feet, then, that my aunt had conquered all her prejudices, and determined to buy my happiness at the cost of her pride. I prayed earnestly, joyfully, kissing the very spot at the foot which once before I had kissed in gratitude and love, and then went back to my post. Germain was defending himself valiantly against the marchioness and M. de Tourmagne. He thanked Madame la Marquise very much; he was honored, touched; he was most grateful; he blushed to refuse such goodness, but he could not accept.

"I know what I am offering you," urged my aunt, desiring to prolong the scene which exactly suited her heart and her spirit; "I assure you the young lady is both pretty and well brought up."

"Rather giddy in the head," said M. de Tourmagne, wickedly, turning towards my door, "but a very good heart; can read a serious book and keep a secret; a very fair specimen of an agreeable young person, on the whole."

"She deserves some one better than I am," said poor Germain.

"I may also tell you," said my aunt, "that she has already seen you, and, I have reason to believe, she would not have the slightest objection to you."

"Stephanie knows her," said M. de Tourmagne, in his most careless manner, "and she has found out that Madame Darcet would rather like the match."

"Mademoiselle Stephanie is too good," said Germain with a little tremble in his voice; "but I assure you, Madame la Marquise, and you, my dear friend, that my resolution is unalterable. I cannot, I must not marry,"

"Monsieur Darcet," said my aunt, emphatically, "I am so convinced that this marriage would be happy for both of you, without mentioning your friends, that I will not give up the idea until you have seen the girl for yourself. She is here, for she dined with us to-day; and I shall go and fetch her."

"Oh! I implore you, madame!" cried her victim, in despair; "do nothing of the kind."

"Yes, yes," laughed Madame d'Aubecourt, coming towards my hiding-place, "I must really see if you love stones and hieroglyphics so distractedly as that they have no rival."

Then, while poor Germain looked around, as if for some means of escape, she glided in and caught me in her arms. I drew her to the prie-dieu and pointed silently to the bronze crucifix.

"Did you recognize it?" she whispered.

"Yes," I said, "and I knew that I had a mother here as well as in heaven."

. "Dear child, she said, "I am quite as happy and content as you are. But come, we must not lose time."

I trembled violently, but she wound her arms firmly round my waist, and led me out into the dazzling light of the *salon*. M. de Tourmagne looked extremely excited, and Germain was so dazed and confused that he did not look up at all.

"Well," said M. de Tourmagne, catching his arm; "look at her. Now will you stay?"

He gazed at me then as if he could hardly believe his eyes. He turned fearfully pale, and looked from me to my aunt with such an appealing look, that she was half-frightened. "This is she," she said, almost sobbing. We had come quite close to him; I put one of my hands on his, and whispered brokenly: "Mother, when I am big enough, I will marry Germain."

"Rœschen!" he cried, rapturously, snatching me from my aunt's arm. "Oh! mademoiselle, I did not think I had loved you so long."

"Come, come," said my aunt, after a few happy minutes, "we must not keep all the happiness to ourselves. My dear Germain, allow poor Rœschen to recover a little from her emotions, and run home and bring us your dear mother and sister."

Oh! may God be thanked, dearest Elise!

THE END.

www.ingramcontent.com/pod-product-compliance
Lightning Source LLC
Chambersburg PA
CBHW020608030726
47497CB00007B/2147